DISNEY

MARY
POPPINS
RETURNS

For information about permission to reproduce selections from
this book, write to trade.permissions@hmhco.com or to Permissions,
Houghton Mifflin Harcourt Publishing Company, 3 Park Avenue,
19th Floor, New York, New York 10016.

hmhco.com

ISBN: 978-1-328-51274-1

Printed in the United States of America
DOC 10 9 8 7 6 5 4 3 2 1
4500733329

Disney
MARY POPPINS RETURNS

Adapted by KATHY McCULLOUGH

Screenplay by DAVID MAGEE

Based on the series of books by P. L. TRAVERS

Houghton Mifflin Harcourt

Boston   New York

CHAPTER 1

It was a dreary morning in London. Gray clouds filled the sky, and mist covered the streets. In the winter of 1934, the mood of the city matched the weather. Jobs were hard to find—and fair wages were even harder to garner. Parents labored to feed their families, and the lines outside the soup kitchens seemed to grow longer every day.

But one particular Londoner never forgot that behind those clouds was a bright sun, ready to shine. His name was Jack, and he was a lamplighter. It was his task each evening to bicycle through his assigned section of town and use a long lit pole, which looked like a very tall

match, to light the gas-powered streetlamps that illuminated the sidewalks, avenues, parks, and city squares.

But lighting the lamps was only half his job. Just as
important—and in some ways more vital, as far as Jack
was concerned—was to make his rounds again in the
morning. During the early hours of dawn, Jack would
repeat his route, but this time he would travel with a
ladder instead of a pole. He'd use the ladder to climb to
the top of each streetlamp and extinguish the gas flame
inside.

Jack didn't mind the cold and damp on this winter
morning. He'd layered a gray wool jacket over his cot-
ton shirt and red knitted vest, and he had tugged a gray
wool cap tight over his choppy brown hair. His hands
were bare, since gloves didn't pair well with gas flames.
It was Sunday, a day off for some. But for others, like the
news vendors, policemen, and lamplighters, every day
was a workday. Luckily, Jack loved his job.

Jack sped around a corner and onto the Victoria
Embankment, a wide path that ran alongside the River
Thames. Ahead in the distance, the tall majestic clock
tower known as Big Ben, named after the giant bell
inside, rose above the horizon. The hands of the dial on

its glowing face inched toward eight o'clock, when the bell inside the tower would toll, ringing out over the city to announce another hour had passed.

Not yet doused, the streetlamps along the walls of the river stood at attention as Jack glided past. Their flickering gas flames were reflected in the softly rippling current of the river, making it seem as if each lamp had a more whimsical twin who swayed and blinked over the surface of the water while its sibling on land remained serious and still.

Jack smiled at the sight and continued on, arriving at the first of his assigned streetlamps. He parked his bike, unhooked the ladder from the bike's back, and leaned the ladder against the streetlamp. After climbing to the top, he lifted the latch that opened one of the glass windows of the lamp. He then reached in and turned a knob to lower the flame, which grew softer and smaller until it faded away. Jack then closed and re-latched the lamp's glass door and climbed down.

Why was this job, of dimming the lights, just as important as lighting the lamps—or maybe even more important? Because when the lamps were lit each evening, they signaled the end of the day, a time to set aside unfulfilled goals and unfinished tasks. But in the morning, each extinguished light announced to the world that there was a fresh new day ahead. There was now time to fulfill those earlier goals—or set new ones. Morning meant a new future filled with possibilities. Whenever a new day dawned, there was no telling what incredible adventures lay ahead.

Jack continued on his rounds, taking in the sights and sounds and smells of the city. He swerved around a trio of street urchins who were chasing after a coal truck and snatching up the lumps of coal that tumbled off its back. He raced past newspaper vendors opening their stands for the day and fruit carts with their bright, bracing smells of fresh apples and ripening pears. He zoomed through a flock of pigeons pecking at crumbs in the square outside St. Paul's Cathedral. The birds scattered and flapped their wings, taking off into the air with a *wicka-wicka-WHOOSH!*

Jack observed the down-turned faces and hunched shoulders of his fellow Londoners as he cycled past and called out cheerful greetings to them. With each "Hullo!" he shouted, he received a startled look, but the look was almost always followed by a smile. He enjoyed seeing the faces of strangers light up, the mental fog of sleep washing away, replaced by excitement about the day ahead.

At last Jack reached his favorite neighborhood. Pretty tan brick town houses lined the quiet streets; an iron fence surrounded the matchbox garden in front of each residence. At one end of the neighborhood stood a lush park, with a walkway along its periphery and another walkway through it, where people could stroll. Jack cut through the park on his bicycle and passed the park-keeper, a gruff man who wore a perpetual scowl, one Jack had yet to transform into a smile.

"Morning!" Jack shouted to the park-keeper, doffing his cap. The park-keeper, however, barely glanced up as he stabbed his poker into a piece of trash and deposited it into a nearby bin.

Jack exited the park and headed onto Cherry Tree Lane. He'd not only known the houses here since he was very young, but he knew the families as well— especially one family. Number 17 Cherry Tree Lane was the home of the Banks family. When Jack was just a lad, he would wave up to young Jane and Michael Banks as they smiled down to him each day from their bedroom window on the second floor.

Now Jane and Michael had grown up. Jane lived in another part of town, but Michael still lived in the same house and had children of his own—three of them.

"Hello, Jack!" yelled Annabel Banks as she leaned out the second-floor window.

"Hello!" echoed her twin brother, John, who appeared next to her. John looked much like Jack remembered Michael having looked: dark-haired and serious. Annabel bore a closer resemblance to her aunt as a girl, with her freckled face and reddish-brown hair.

Jack parked his bike and waved up to them both. "Hullo! Everything all right, children?"

They nodded and disappeared back inside as Jack set up his ladder next to the streetlamp in front of the town house. He glanced toward the rooftop next door as he climbed.

Admiral Boom, a retired ship's admiral, had lived on Cherry Tree Lane longer than the Banks family had, and he had re-created his former ship on the roof of his house. Huge masts rose toward the sky, and the bow jutted out over the street. Parked on the ship's deck was a working cannon, which the admiral fired off each hour to mark the time.

From the top of his ladder, Jack could just see Big Ben in the distance. It was very nearly eight o'clock. The admiral was usually on the roof by now, sitting in his wheelchair next to his cannon, with First Mate Mr. Binnacle standing at attention beside him.

A moment later, Admiral Boom appeared, pushed in his wheelchair by Mr. Binnacle. Admiral Boom was in uniform, as always, his cap perched neatly on his head and his mutton-chop sideburns freshly trimmed.

Mr. Binnacle, who was in his navy-blue sailor's pea-coat, parked the wheelchair and crossed to the edge of the roof. He blew a loud whistle. "Admiral above deck!" he called out, alerting the neighbors.

Jack saluted the two navy men. First Mate Binnacle and the admiral returned the salute. Jack smiled. All was right with the world, as it was every fresh new morning. He returned the ladder to his bicycle and pedaled off, content that the Banks family and the rest of the residents on Cherry Tree Lane were happy and well. He turned the corner and therefore didn't see the unfamiliar black car pulling up to the curb in front of number 17.

CHAPTER 2

Inside the Bankses' home, things were not as tranquil as they were outside. Jane had paid an early-morning visit to her brother, on the pretense that she was just passing by on her way to work. She'd taken to visiting more often in the past year, ever since Michael's wife, Kate, had died. Jane knew her brother was having a hard time adjusting to life as a single father. He'd had to give up painting and take a job at the bank. It was work that didn't come naturally to one with his artistic inclinations.

She and Michael were in the parlor when they heard a scream from the kitchen. They rushed into the front entrance hallway just as Ellen, the family housekeeper, burst through the kitchen door, dripping wet.

"The bloomin' sink's exploded!" Ellen exclaimed, waving an arm toward the kitchen and sending drops of water into Michael's and Jane's eyes.

"Not *again*," Michael groaned. He wiped his eyes and hurried into the kitchen, where he found water spraying from both taps, like a pair of mini-fountains. Water dripped from the cabinets and cascaded off the counters onto the flooded floor. Michael put one arm over his face to protect himself from the geysers and reached out to turn off the taps: the right one shut off, but the left handle broke off in his hand.

Michael lowered his arm and watched as water gurgled out of the top of the left tap, now less like a geyser than a waterfall. In the past six months, he'd battled four different leaks in the kitchen, not to mention the leaks in the upstairs bathrooms. When would it end?

Michael sighed. He set the broken brass handle down on the waterlogged counter and began opening drawers. He'd left a wrench in there—somewhere!

In the hallway, Ellen wrung out her damp apron, creating a puddle on the floor. "I told 'im to get them pipes fixed," she told Jane. "They been there since the Romans ruled."

Jane gave Ellen a sympathetic smile. "Why don't you fetch a mop and some towels, and I'll help you clean up."

Ellen nodded and opened the narrow door next to the kitchen under the staircase. She sighed and trudged down the steps to the cellar.

A moment later, Annabel and John hurried down from upstairs, having heard the commotion. "I'll ring the plumbers," Annabel told her aunt.

"I'll turn off the water at the mains," John said. Plumbing problems were a familiar event, and the twins had had a lot of practice at doing what needed to be done. As John raced down the steps after Ellen, Annabel crossed to the phone on the hall side table, picked up the receiver, and dialed, having learned the plumbers' number by heart.

Jane nodded at her capable niece and nephew. She was impressed with both of them but sad they'd had to take on so much responsibility over the past year. Jane tried to help out when she could, but it was more than she could keep up with, due to her own job and her volunteer work.

Jane pushed through the kitchen door and gathered up all the kitchen towels she could find. "Let's wait for the professionals, shall we?" she told her brother, holding out a towel and offering him a smile. She knew that finding the humor amid an unfolding disaster always made it easier to endure.

Michael took the towel but didn't smile back.

Meanwhile, two men had emerged from the mysterious black car parked in front of the Bankses' town house. One of the men was young and slim, dressed in a pin-striped suit that fit him perfectly. The other man had flecks of gray in his hair, and while the vest of his suit seemed to be a little snug on his round figure, the jacket appeared too loose, as if he'd bought the wrong size in both areas. The older man wore round-framed eyeglasses, which had a tendency to slide down his nose.

The men waited at the car a moment, glancing toward Big Ben in the distance. Finally, the minute hand on the grand clock tower reached twelve and the bell tolled, chiming eight times. The two men took out their pocket watches and adjusted them to match the time on the clock.

Next door, on the roof sporting the re-created vessel, Admiral Boom grumbled, furious. "Great steaming clams, they've done it again!" the admiral exclaimed to First Mate Binnacle. "Those blundering blowfish have rung Big Ben too soon!"

Mr. Binnacle nodded, even though he knew Big Ben was never wrong. The admiral, on the other hand, had slowed down in his later years, and his sense of time had slowed with him. Mr. Binnacle would never dare correct the admiral, however. Admiral Boom was his commander. This meant that for Mr. Binnacle it was not eight o'clock until the admiral declared it so.

Down on the street, the two men had returned their watches to their pockets and were now heading up the steps of number 17.

Inside the house, Annabel was still on the phone, waiting for the plumbers to answer. She then spotted her little brother, Georgie, trudging down the stairs.

"What's happening?" asked Georgie. He hugged his stuffed giraffe, Gillie, in his arms and jumped down from the final stair to the floor, causing his overgrown blond bangs to flop against his forehead.

Annabel held up her hand, signaling Georgie to stop.

"Don't go in the kitchen," she warned him. "Not without your wellies."

Georgie looked at Annabel, confused. Why would he need his rain boots in the kitchen?

But Annabel had returned her focus to the phone. "Yes, hello," she said into the receiver. "We've had a burst pipe."

Now Georgie understood: the kitchen was flooded. What fun! He'd had a lovely time sloshing about when the bathtub pipes burst in the children's bathroom the month before. He tried to remember if he'd left his rain boots upstairs, but his thoughts were interrupted by a tap on the front door.

"Excuse me," Annabel said into the phone. She put her hand over the receiver and called behind her toward the open cellar door. "Ellen, could you please get the door? I've got the plumbers here!"

Ellen emerged from the cellar holding the mop and towels. She glanced toward the door with surprise. The plumbers were at the house already? "That was quick work!" she said. She spotted the youngest Banks child at the foot of the stairs. "Here, Georgie. Take these." She dropped the towels into Georgie's arms. He struggled to balance the large load and not let go of Gillie, who did not like to be dropped on his head—although this did sometimes occur.

Ellen plodded to the front door, mop in hand. "All right, all right," she grumbled as the tapping continued. "I'm coming." She opened the door to reveal the two men from the car standing on the steps, nailing a notice to the doorframe.

"Good morning, ma'am," said the older man in a nasally voice that made him sound as if he was getting over a cold.

"They don't look like plumbers," Ellen called over her shoulder to Annabel.

"I meant I had the plumbers on the phone," explained Annabel, pointing to the receiver.

"We are not plumbers," said the older man, clearly offended. "I am Mr. Hamilton Gooding, and this is Mr. Templeton Frye. We are lawyers."

"Lawyers?" Ellen frowned, disappointed. "Here I was hopin' you'd prove useful." She handed the mop to Mr. Gooding and closed the door in his face.

"Water's off!" John called up from the cellar.

Annabel hung up the phone. "And the plumbers are on their way."

Jane emerged from the kitchen, brushing the water off the front of her dress. "Well done, everyone," she said. "Whew! Such excitement!"

Georgie peered around the tower of towels in his arms, having heard his aunt's voice. "What are you doing here, Aunt Jane?" he asked.

Jane took a towel from the top of the pile. She patted her face and dried her hands. "We're giving out breakfast at the union hall," she explained. This was one of her many volunteer tasks. "I snuck away for morning hugs." She threw the damp towel over her shoulder and leaned down to hug her youngest nephew, taking the towels from his arms as she straightened up. "Thank you for these. They'll be very useful for sopping up."

Georgie followed his aunt into the kitchen. He'd given up on the idea of looking for his wellies now that the sopping up was about to begin. He didn't want to miss a chance to slosh about, even if his feet did get wet.

Meanwhile, the tapping outside had resumed. John shot Annabel a questioning look. Annabel shrugged. She hadn't been listening to Ellen's brief conversation with the men and had assumed they'd gone away. But apparently that was not the case.

Ellen once again opened the door to find the two men. "Will you stop that bangin'?" she barked at them. "It's barely eight o'clock on a Sunday mornin'!" She noticed Mr. Gooding holding her mop and snatched it back from him. How on earth had that happened? "Say, wot'cher doin' with me mop?"

"Forgive the intrusion, ma'am," said Mr. Frye. "Our current workload prevents us taking weekends off."

Mr. Gooding pushed up his glasses. "We would like to have a word with Mr. Banks, if he is available," he said.

Ellen finally noticed the paper the men had nailed to the doorframe. "'Repossession'?" she read with alarm.

Mr. Frye nodded nervously. Unlike his colleague, he truly hated this part of their work. Each expression of horror, shock, or despair he saw on a person's face when they realized their home was to be taken away gave him a sharp stab of guilt. With each notice they nailed up, he made a silent wish that the family inside could and would find a way out of their situation.

However, it wasn't horror or despair but contempt he saw on the housekeeper's face. "Wait here," she told the lawyers, giving them each a lethal glare. "Mr. Banks!"

she called out as she marched past the twins to the kitchen.

Annabel and John exchanged looks. They knew things had gotten bad since their mother's death, but this couldn't be right. The notice must be a mistake. It was the wrong house, the wrong family. If Mr. Frye had been able to see the twins' faces, he would have seen shock and worry in their expressions.

Georgie exited the kitchen, happily squeezing the water between his toes inside his wet slippers. He spotted the lawyers and peered at them curiously. Mr. Frye gave the little boy a wave. Georgie smiled and waved back.

John quickly darted over to his brother. He didn't want Georgie to know anything about what was happening. He was too young. John nodded to Annabel, who quickly joined him.

The twins took Georgie's hands and led him upstairs. He grinned as his wet slippers squeaked delightfully on the steps. He didn't notice John glancing over the railing toward the kitchen door with an anxious look that pleaded for his father to come out, speak to the lawyers, and make everything right.

CHAPTER
3

Ellen entered the kitchen and glanced around at the mess. "Looks like the River Thames in here," she said to Michael and Jane.

"Don't worry," Michael told Ellen, taking the mop out of her hand. "We'll finish up. Why don't you see to breakfast?"

Ellen shrugged. "S'pose someone has to—'less we all want to starve." She disappeared into the walk-in pantry at the far end of the kitchen.

"Why don't you let Ellen clean up?" Jane whispered to Michael.

"I'm afraid lately that means more work for me,"

Michael replied. Ellen had become more and more forgetful over the past few years, and since Kate's death, her absentmindedness had gotten even worse. "The other day I found a butcher's sack hanging on the coatrack—and my hat was in the pantry."

"Are you sure it's not time we thought about moving her over to her sister's?" Jane asked. The last thing Michael needed right then was another person to have to look after.

"Ellen is family," Michael said firmly. "She stays here."

"You're right," Jane said, silently vowing to come by more often. It would be difficult to find the time, but she'd figure out a way.

Ellen popped out from the pantry. "'Scuse me, sir. I plum forgot. The wolves are at the door." She jerked her head toward the front hallway.

At first, Michael feared Ellen not only had become more forgetful but had begun to see things as well— until he peered through the kitchen doorway and spotted the two men waiting on the front steps.

"What do they want?" Michael asked.

Ellen let out a disdainful snort. "A good thrashin', if

you ask me," she said, and then disappeared back into the pantry.

Michael exited the kitchen, followed by his sister. Jane ran a hand through her hair and felt a tangle in it. "Oh, my!" she said when she glanced into the hall mirror. "I look a fright." She always tried to look nice for the people who came to the union hall to get a meal. It showed respect for them and their situation. "I'll be right down." She headed upstairs to borrow a hairbrush from her niece.

Michael had arrived at the door, the mop still in his hands. "I'm so sorry," he told the men, and gestured for them to come in. "We're struggling through a bit of chaos this morning."

Mr. Gooding stepped into the hallway and gave the damp Michael a disdainful once-over. "So it seems," he said. He waved impatiently for Mr. Frye to enter. "Unfortunately, Mr. Banks," Mr. Gooding continued, "our business cannot wait."

Michael nodded toward the parlor, indicating that the men should enter. But just as he was about to follow them in, Ellen ducked her head out from the kitchen. "Excuse me, sir," she said. "How exactly am I supposed to make breakfast when there's nothing in the pantry but pickled herring and marmalade?"

"I like pickled herring and marmalade," Georgie called out from the stairs. He had snuck away from his brother and sister, determined to get more sloshing in before the kitchen mess was completely cleaned up.

"The groceries!" Michael said, slamming his palm to his forehead. "I meant to go yesterday." It seemed Ellen wasn't the only one who had become more forgetful lately.

"Give me the list, sir," Ellen said. "I'll go."

"No!" Michael said quickly.

Annabel and John, who were running downstairs after the escaped Georgie, immediately echoed his protest. The twins were well aware of Ellen's frequent bouts of absentmindedness. The last time she'd gone out for apples and butter to make a pie, she'd come home with a packet of geranium seeds, two hammers, and several tins of sardines. Who knew what she'd end up bringing home this time?

"Nearly everything's closed today anyway," Michael told Ellen, relieved to have thought up an excuse that wouldn't hurt her feelings.

"Very well, then," Ellen said with a shrug. "Pickled herring for breakfast, marmalade for lunch."

Once Ellen had disappeared back into the kitchen, John stepped over to his father. "That little shop across the park will be open," he whispered. "The three of us can go after breakfast."

"That would be wonderful, John," Michael said, grateful.

"But you said we would go to the park today!" Georgie protested, tugging on Annabel's sleeve.

"We'll cut through the park on the way," Annabel told him, taking his hand. "Come along. Let's get you dressed for breakfast." She led her little brother back upstairs.

John took the mop from Michael. "I'll take that, Father."

"Thank you," Michael said.

After his father had gone into the parlor, John mopped up the footprints Georgie and the grown-ups had made in the hall. He was determined to have the hall and kitchen floors completely dry before his brother and sister came back down—even though Georgie would be disappointed.

"What can I do for you?" John heard his father ask the two strangers. John would have liked to hear their reply, but he'd finished in the hallway, and his brother and sister would be heading down any moment. So he carried the mop off to the kitchen. He didn't see his aunt coming down the stairs.

Inside the parlor, the two lawyers were introducing themselves. "We're solicitors with the law firm of Gordy, Cordry, Gooding and Frye," said Mr. Gooding. Before he could continue, he heard a laugh from the doorway and turned to see Jane in the hall. She had just put on her coat and was struggling to suppress a giggle. Mr. Gooding glared at her.

"Sorry," she said, letting out a small laugh. She couldn't help it. The name of the law firm sounded like a verse from a silly Mother Goose rhyme.

Mr. Gooding squinted at a large button pinned to the lapel of Jane's coat. It was imprinted with the word SPRUCE. "'Spruce'?" he asked. "Is that your garden club?"

Jane's smile vanished. She was annoyed when men assumed the only activities women took part in involved gardening, cooking, or cleaning. "No," she told him. "It stands for the Society for the Protection of the

Rights of the Underpaid Citizens of England."

"A *labor organizer?*" Mr. Gooding peered at Jane over the top of his glasses with a look of disapproval. He had no use for unions, what with their nonstop talk and pursuit of enacting fair wages and humane hours for the less fortunate and underprivileged. If people wanted to make more money and work decent hours, they should know well enough to be born to wealthy families and graduate from prestigious schools.

"Yes," Jane said, proud of her work. "We also run soup kitchens and organize clothing drives, among other activities that aid the poor and working class. It's a never-ending job these days."

Mr. Frye nodded sympathetically. He thought of all the people they'd evicted—hard workers who had lost their savings due to an illness in the family or to their place of business closing down. Unlike his colleague, he knew one couldn't just *choose* to be rich. "I'm sure it is, Mrs. Banks," he told Jane.

"Miss Banks, actually," Jane said, correcting him. "I'm Michael's sister."

"My wife passed away this past year," Michael explained.

"That's awful!" exclaimed Mr. Frye. He remembered the little boy who had waved at him. "Your poor children."

Mr. Gooding nodded stiffly. "Our deepest condolences," he said.

"Thank you," replied Michael. "So, what brings the two of you here this morning?"

Mr. Gooding adjusted his glasses as he referred to a small notebook in his hand. It was where he kept the list of foreclosures and evictions. "According to our records, Mr. Banks, you took out a loan with Fidelity Fiduciary Bank last year against the value of your home."

"You did *what?*" Jane asked Michael. She waited for him to deny it, to declare there must have been a clerical error at the bank. Instead he said, "I had to, Jane. I didn't have any choice, what with Kate, and the bills piling up—"

"Yes, well," Mr. Gooding interrupted. The visit had already gone on much longer than he had scheduled. "It seems you've fallen three months behind in payments, and now the bank has retained our firm to collect what you owe."

"I *am* sorry," Michael told the lawyers. "Kate, my late

wife, used to handle all our finances, and I've been a bit off my stride." He sat down at a small desk at the side of the parlor and removed his checkbook from the front drawer. "How much is it I owe you exactly?"

"Unfortunately, the bank is now demanding you pay back the entire loan in full," Mr. Gooding said, relieved finally to get to the point of the visit.

Michael looked up from the desk in shock. "The entire loan? That's more than I make in a year! I couldn't possibly."

When Jane heard this, her stomach sank. She'd hoped it was just a small loan Michael had taken out—small enough that she could easily help cover it and pay it back. But a loan as large as Michael's annual salary meant he owed thousands of pounds.

"Oh, dear!" Mr. Frye said. Like Jane, he'd been secretly hoping the loan could be easily paid back. Mr. Gooding gave Mr. Frye a sideways glance and shook his head in disapproval. Mr. Gooding had told Mr. Frye time and again that it wasn't businesslike to show emotion. Mr. Frye, chastened, nodded and bit his lip.

Mr. Gooding returned to the business at hand. "You have five days," he told Michael. "If you are unable to pay in full by Friday at midnight, I'm afraid we'll have to repossess your home, and you will have to vacate the premises."

Michael was stunned. He could be evicted? Surely they couldn't do that. There'd been no warning. And this was his house, the house he had grown up in. It couldn't just be taken away.

Could it?

CHAPTER 4

"**B**ut I work at Fidelity Fiduciary," Michael told the lawyers. He was sure being an employee of the bank that had made the loan had to count for something.

Mr. Gooding let out an amused sniff. "Not as an accountant, I presume," he said.

Michael didn't seem to notice Mr. Gooding's sarcasm. "No, as a teller. I took a part-time position there this past year. You see, I'm really an artist—"

"Be that as it may . . ." Mr. Gooding said, interrupting again. He really didn't think he needed to say more. He signaled Mr. Frye that it was time to go. Their message had been delivered and it was long past time to move on to the next house.

But Michael wasn't ready to give up. "Our father, George Banks, was a senior partner at Fidelity Fiduciary," Michael said. He couldn't imagine the bank seizing the home of one of its former partners.

Unfortunately, it was clear from Mr. Gooding's terse shake of the head that this fact was of no help.

Jane had been listening to the conversation with growing dismay, but when Michael mentioned their father, it triggered a memory. "Father left us bank shares!" she said to Michael. "You could use them to pay off the loan."

Michael brightened. He'd forgotten about the shares. He'd been saving them for the children, for their futures—but right then, keeping a roof over their heads was more important.

Mr. Frye, too, perked up, relieved that—for this family, at least—eviction might be avoided. "They have shares in the bank!" he said to Mr. Gooding with a smile. "That does change things, doesn't it?"

Mr. Gooding scowled. The day was not going at all as planned, and when his day did not go as planned, he grew very irritated. He peered over his glasses at Michael. "You have the shares certificate?" he asked.

Michael turned to Jane, confused by the question.

"Sorry?" Jane said to the men. "The what?"

Mr. Frye made the shape of a rectangle in the air with his fingers. "The document," he said.

"The document proving you own shares in the bank," Mr. Gooding said impatiently.

"I suppose it must be somewhere among Father's old papers," Michael said to Jane.

Before Jane could reply, a loud *BOOM!* shook the walls. Objects on the shelves rattled and the paintings . on the wall were knocked askew. The lawyers clutched each other, terrified, as ash flew out of the fireplace. "Good heavens!" Mr. Gooding said, coughing. "Are you housing anarchists?" He let go of Mr. Frye and watched, dumbfounded, as Michael and Jane calmly replaced the fallen objects and pushed the furniture back into place, neither of them at all startled by the blast.

"That was the admiral, next door," Jane explained. "He fires up a cannon to mark the hour."

Mr. Gooding and Mr. Frye checked their pocket watches. "But he's over fifteen minutes late," said Mr. Frye.

"I'm afraid he's been running a little behind these last few years," Michael said.

"As are *we* this morning." Mr. Gooding snapped his watch closed, not bothering to add that Michael and his unruly household were to blame for this tardiness. He handed Michael a copy of the repossession document. "You've been given notice," he said. "Good day to you both. We'll see ourselves out." Mr. Gooding moved briskly to the front hall. "Come along, Mr. Frye," he called behind him.

"I hope you find that shares certificate," Mr. Frye told Jane and Michael. "I really do." He gave them an encouraging smile and followed his colleague out.

Jane straightened the last few tilted pictures on the wall as Michael stared down at the notice. "Why didn't you tell me you'd taken out a loan?" she asked her brother.

Michael set the notice on the desk, avoiding her eyes. "I didn't want to worry you—or the children. I kept thinking I could catch up. Kate always managed." He picked up a small framed photo that had tipped over during the cannon blast. It was of a pretty young woman with a warm smile and an obvious resemblance to Georgie and the twins. "I can't lose our home," he said softly. "She's everywhere." He placed the photo on the desk and gazed around the room, which was filled with memories of the days and nights they'd spent there as a family. "I can't lose her again."

Jane crossed to Michael and wrapped her arms around him from behind. "We won't let that happen," she told her brother. "But you know we don't have the money between us, which means we have to find that shares certificate." She straightened up. "Where do you think Father might have kept it?"

"Up in the attic, I suppose," Michael said. He spun around to face his sister. "But I don't want to bring you into my problems."

"This is our family home," Jane said. "And you're about to lose it. So stop keeping things from me, and stop pretending everything's fine."

"Are we going to lose our home?"

Michael and Jane turned to see Georgie, who had entered the dining room adjoining the parlor from the kitchen. Annabel and John stood behind him. It was clear the three had heard everything.

Michael rushed over to Georgie and gave him a

quick hug. "Of course not," he assured the children. "Everything's fine."

"But you just said we don't have enough money," Georgie protested.

"Well, I can make more," Michael said. He returned to the desk and drew a piece of stationery from one of the drawers. "I'm a banker now, aren't I?" He quickly made a sketch on the paper. "That's what bankers do—make money."

"But you're not a banker," Georgie said. "You're a painter."

"Painters don't make money," Michael said. "Not these days." He handed Georgie the finished sketch. "There, you see? The day has hardly begun and I've already made you ten pounds."

Georgie stared at the sketch, amazed. His father had created an actual ten-pound note! All he needed to do was draw hundreds more and they'd be rich!

Annabel and John were no longer young enough to be fooled by Michael's sketch, however, or by his false cheer. But they put on brave faces for their father's sake.

"We'd best be on our way," John said. He checked his pocket watch. They needed to get the shopping done as quickly and efficiently as possible. This would make one less thing their father would have to worry about.

Michael handed John several coins. "Georgie shouldn't have to spend his ten pounds on the shopping," Michael said with a wink.

Annabel smiled at the joke, but John just nodded and pocketed the money. "Thank you, Father," he said.

Jane helped the children with their coats and hats, and after they'd left, she took off her own coat and hung it back on the rack. "Shall we search the attic, then?" she asked her brother.

Michael stared at her in surprise. "Don't you have to go to work?"

Jane rolled up her sleeves and headed up the stairs. "Work can wait."

Michael shook his head and followed. He'd always been impressed by his down-to-earth sister. She had a lot in common with the twins. Like Kate, all three always seemed to know what to do—and never hesitated when it came to getting something done. "Thank you, Jane," he said when they reached the top of the stairs. "I'll look in the attic. Why don't you check Father's old wardrobe?"

Jane smiled, gave him a salute, and headed off to the spare room, where some of their parents' old furniture was kept. Michael reached up to a latch in the ceiling and pulled it down, revealing a ladder that led to the attic on the third floor. He took a breath and began to climb, determined to remain as optimistic as Jane.

They would find the certificate, he told himself. They would.

CHAPTER
5

Although there were still plenty of clouds in the sky as the three Banks children made their way toward the park entrance, a fresh breeze had arrived and chased the fog away. Several of the Bankses' neighbors from Cherry Tree Lane were out for their Sunday-morning stroll. Georgie spotted Miss Lark, one of their wealthier neighbors, walking her black-and-tan dog, Willoughby.

"Miss Lark!" Georgie called out. He pulled his hands free from the twins' grasp and dashed ahead of them. Miss Lark was kind and quite fond of the Banks family. She stopped to let Georgie scratch Willoughby behind his ears.

As the twins made their way toward their brother, Annabel read through the shopping list and John counted the coins their father had given them.

"Father didn't give us enough, did he?" Annabel asked her brother.

John shook his head. "Not nearly."

"We'll ask for bruised plums at half off," Annabel told him. "That's what Mother used to do."

John nodded and gave his sister a grateful smile. He was thankful that Annabel was as responsible as he was. It made the job of taking care of their family a little easier. It was also a relief to have someone to confide in. "What if Father does lose the house?" he asked her.

"We'll just have to figure out a way to get it back," Annabel said. She took John's hand and squeezed it.

John squeezed back. "You're right. That's what Mother would have done."

At the Bankses' house, Michael sat down on the floor of the attic in front of one of the dozens of packed crates crowding the room. He'd already searched through his father's old desk, opening every drawer and examining each piece of paper inside. But he'd found nothing resembling a bank certificate. What he had found was a lot of old bills and worthless canceled checks, all of which he had tossed into an empty box he was using as a rubbish bin.

The attic had already been a mess, even before Michael's search commenced. It had been that way for some time. Michael had moved his easels, canvases, and art supplies up to the attic after Kate had died—and he had shoved them into a corner. The children's old cradles were propped up on top of tables that needed fixing, and Jane's and his childhood belongings were scattered here and there: they ranged from broken sports equipment and dust-covered dolls to bicycles with missing wheels. It was as if the attic was a storage room for memories— lost times from the past, tossed together in no particular order and then locked away.

Michael lifted a faded quilt out of the crate before him. Beneath it he discovered a worn leather jewelry box. The box had a *K* monogrammed on the lid, and when he opened it, a graceful melody played. Inside the box was a delicate silver necklace, the one Michael had given to Kate on their first anniversary. He lifted it out, remembering how Kate would roll the chain between her fingers when she was lost in thought.

He gripped the necklace in his hand and pressed his fist into his chest. There were so many memories of Kate there in the attic, and in the rest of the house. And he missed so much about her: the way she'd tease him about his worries; the way she'd joke with the children, filling the house with laughter. If only he could go back to those days.

He opened his hand and raised the necklace up to the dim light filtering in from the dusty attic windows. The silver chain swayed and sparkled. "Oh, Kate," he said softly. "You'd know just what to do. I know you would." The box played its soft melody in reply.

Michael shook his head, attempting to shake off his melancholy. He couldn't go back in time any more than he could stop the children from growing up. He knew this. John and Annabel were always so serious now. He knew they worried about him, but it wasn't right for children to worry about their father.

The certificate, the certificate, he reminded himself, and gently returned the necklace to the jewelry box.

Finding the bank certificate was the most important thing right then. As head of the Banks household, he had a responsibility to his family—many responsibilities. And in order to carry out those responsibilities, he needed to have a house to keep hold of.

"Nothing in the wardrobe," Jane called out from the hall below. Michael could hear the steps of the ladder creaking as she began to climb. He quickly closed the jewelry box and wiped his eyes, then pushed the crate of Kate's things away just as Jane's head popped up from the opening in the floor. "Oh, my goodness," she said, taking in the cluttered space.

Michael smiled. "Yes, it's quite a mess, isn't it?"

"Have you looked in Father's old desk?" she asked.

Michael nodded. "Just rubbish," he told her, gesturing to the overflowing box of discarded papers.

Jane climbed the rest of the way up to join Michael. She circled the room, amazed at how well attics were able to store snapshots of people's lives. She took one look at Georgie's old cradle and instantly pictured him when he was just days old, blinking up at the world through sleepy new eyes.

Jane reached Michael's art supplies and lifted up a

paintbrush, stiff and brittle from the dried paint that was never wiped off it. "What are all your art things doing up here?" she asked.

Michael shrugged. "I wasn't using them." He pulled another crate toward him. "There's no joy for me in it anymore. I should probably get rid of it all."

Jane glanced at her brother, hunched over the crate. She knew he couldn't mean that, but she also knew he had more pressing concerns than having to put his art career on hold.

She sat down across from him and helped him lift off the top of the crate. Michael reached in and pulled out a snow globe. Inside the glass oval, a pair of children sat on a sleigh, frozen midway down a hill. "I honestly don't know why we kept most of this stuff," he said.

Jane took the globe from him and tipped it over and back. The tiny white flakes inside floated around the children, creating the illusion that the sleigh was in motion and the children raced down the hill.

Jane smiled and held it up to show Michael, but he'd returned to the crate and was lifting out a tattered handmade kite. Its green paper body was bordered by gold ribbon, but the paper had ripped in several places, rendering it incapable of flying.

"I mean, why on earth did we save *this* old thing?" he asked, frowning at the kite.

Jane smiled and took the kite. "Don't you remember?" She unfurled the suffragette banner that had been tied to the bottom of the frame as a tail. "We used to love flying this kite with Mother and Father." She swooped the kite through the air.

"Well, it won't fly anymore." Before Jane could argue, Michael took the kite from her hands and tossed it into the rubbish box. "Out it goes," he said, ignoring Jane's frown. He stood up, grabbed the box of trash, and carried it to the attic stairs. "It's the future we're concerned with now," he reminded his sister. "No looking back."

Michael set the box of trash next to the rubbish bins in the alley beside the house. He cast a last glance at the old kite, sighed, and then returned to the house to resume the search.

The kite lay atop the discarded papers, not at all

pleased at being called useless. True, it was ripped, and it hadn't loved being cooped up inside a musty old crate in the attic. But at least there had still existed the possibility that one day someone would repair it. Now it seemed destined to end up in the back of a rubbish truck, where it would be crushed beyond recognition— and all hope of flying again would be extinguished.

Nevertheless, it was nice to be outside in the fresh air. The kite tried to enjoy its freedom, feeling the light flutter of its paper as a soft breeze washed over it.

And out on the street, a stronger wind began to blow. It swooped up a handful of leaves and whisked them around in a tiny tornado and then curved around the side of the Bankses' house to the alley. The wind whirled and swirled, making its way closer to the rubbish bins. When it reached the box Michael had brought out, the wind slipped underneath the kite and propelled it upward until the kite was balanced on its base. The kite shuddered as the icy wind batted at it from both sides.

And then, to its astonishment, the kite rose from the box and was carried by the breeze out of the alley and into the street. The kite flew down Cherry Tree Lane, darting past Willoughby, who barked at it in alarm. Miss Lark looked around, but the kite had already raced ahead, the bottom of its diamond frame skittering over the cobblestones as it dodged cars and ducked around passersby.

Jack was riding his bicycle home from his rounds when he spotted the kite popping up from behind a vegetable truck. Jack swerved to the side of the road, braking. He watched, curious, as the kite flew back down to the cobblestones and continued down the street.

Jack raised his eyebrows. The kite definitely seemed to know where it was going—which was odd behavior for a loose kite, as far as Jack was concerned. But Jack had seen a lot of odd things in his life, and he knew they could almost always be explained . . . somehow. He glanced up and noticed the clouds swirling overhead, their movement as purposeful as the kite's. He sensed a frizzle of magic in the air.

Ahead, the kite rounded a corner, disappearing from view. Jack hopped onto his bike and quickly pedaled after it. He had a feeling he knew where it was heading. He smiled, hoping he had guessed right.

CHAPTER
6

Jack followed the kite as it sailed toward the park, sashaying through the entrance gate as if it was just another Londoner out for a Sunday promenade. The kite bounced over the grass for a few feet before catching a gust of wind, which carried it toward a man sitting on a park bench and reading a newspaper. It knocked off the man's hat as it flew over. The hat landed in the man's lap, but the man merely returned the hat to his head without looking up.

No one else in the park paid any attention to the kite, either—except for Jack, still following and trying to keep up. He watched as the kite passed by the Banks children. Annabel was too busy studying the grocery list and John was too busy frowning at his pocket watch for either of them to take notice of the kite. Georgie saw it, however, and his eyes opened wide with wonder. He pulled free of Annabel's hand and chased after it.

"Georgie! Come back!" Annabel and John darted across the grass toward their little brother.

"You two!" the park-keeper shouted at the twins. "Keep off the grass! I don't spend all day caring for it just to see my work trampled on!"

John pointed toward Georgie. "But our brother—"

"You heard me!" the park-keeper barked. *"Now!"* He then waved his rubbish stick at them to emphasize his point.

John and Annabel were too mindful of rules to break one now, especially in front of the angry park-keeper. They returned to the walkway, hurrying along it in the direction Georgie had gone.

Another gust of wind suddenly carried the kite over a thick hedge spanning the park. Georgie reached the hedge, but it was too high to hop over and too long to race around. He had no choice: he had to climb through it. As he waded into the thick brambles, branches scraped through his hair and brushed across his face and hands. When he emerged on the other side, he was covered in leaves and dirt.

A few feet ahead of him, the kite leaned against the arch of a stone bridge. The kite stood motionless, as if it was waiting for Georgie.

Georgie grinned and raced toward the kite. He waited for it to rise up and dart off again, or for another gust of wind to carry it up over the bridge, but things had calmed down and the kite remained still. He reached the bridge and picked up the kite, spotting a spool of thick thread tucked into the back of its frame. He gently pulled it out.

Georgie carried the kite away from the bridge, into an open area on the grass. He held the spool in one hand and lifted the kite with the other, waiting for another breeze to take hold of the kite so he could fly it. In the sky above, the clouds had begun to churn again. A wind high up was hitting the top branches of the park's trees, making them sway and shiver violently.

Georgie felt the kite tremble in his hand as if it was eager to fly again. A second later, the wind plunged down toward them and grabbed the kite, raising it up into the air. Georgie held tight to the spool of string, which quickly unwound.

The kite swam through the air, soaring skyward, and headed for the swirling clouds. The string Georgie gripped unwound completely, but the kite kept rising—and soon Georgie was lifted up as well. He was propelled forward, and although he was only a couple of feet off the ground, he was too afraid to jump down. "Help!" he called out. He gripped the spool for dear life as he was carried over the grass. High above him the kite disappeared into the dark clouds.

Annabel and John had heard Georgie shout. They gazed in the direction of his voice, gasping in horror when they saw their brother rising toward the stormy gray skies.

"We're coming, Georgie!" Annabel called out. This time the twins had no qualms about disobeying the parkkeeper. They raced across the grass and dove through the hedge, determined to rescue their little brother.

Jack had also heard Georgie's cry. He pedaled down the park path and then hopped off his bike, letting it fall to the grass. "Hold on tight!" he yelled as he raced toward Georgie.

Jack grabbed the kite string firmly. He and Georgie pulled on the string with all their might.

Then, suddenly and mysteriously, the sky calmed and the wind slowed. The clouds parted and a figure, holding on to the suffragette banner at the bottom of the kite with a gloved hand, appeared high above them. As the kite started descending, the figure came into view. The twins emerged from the hedge, covered, like Georgie had been, in leaves and dirt. They were just in time to see the figure float slowly and easily to the ground in front of them, her smart shoes making a soft *click* as they hit the pavement.

It was a woman in a blue-and-black striped coat. Her red scarf matched her red gloves and was decorated with black polka dots. The red hat on her head was tilted to one side, and an umbrella was tucked under one arm. In her free hand, she carried a worn carpetbag.

"As I live and breathe . . ." Jack murmured to himself. He'd been right. There *was* magic in the air that day.

John leaned over to Annabel. "Did you just see that?" he asked. Annabel gulped and nodded.

"You need to be more careful when the wind rises, Georgie," the woman said. "You nearly lost your kite." She handed the kite to Jack and then turned to the twins. "And you two nearly lost your Georgie. He might have got away completely if I'd not been holding on to the other end of that string."

The woman circled the three children, frowning at their dirty, wrinkled clothes. The twins were baffled. Had they really seen this woman fly—no, not fly, *float!*—down from the sky?

"My goodness, Annabel," the woman said finally. "You could grow a garden in that much soil." She shook her head at John. "And, John, you're just as filthy."

"How do you know our names?" Annabel asked the mysterious woman.

"Because she's Mary Poppins, of course!" Jack said. He turned to the woman and tipped his cap. "And may I say you look lovely, as always."

"You really think so?" Mary Poppins brushed a speck of dust from her coat and then smiled up at Jack. "It is nice to see you, Jack."

"Good to see you, too, Mary Poppins." He turned to the children. "I was just your age, working for a chimney sweep, when Mary Poppins and I first met." He handed the kite back to Georgie. Now that the wind had died down, there was no danger of Georgie's blowing away.

"How is dear old Bert?" Mary Poppins asked Jack. She remembered the chimney sweep fondly.

"Super, Mary Poppins. Traveling the world, he is." Jack swept out an arm. "Off to points unknown."

Mary Poppins nodded, pleased. "Wonderful. And now *I* am off to speak with the father of these children. This family is in desperate need of a nanny."

Annabel was about to protest, but Mary Poppins waved her hands at the children, shooing them toward the park walkway. "Quick march and best foot forward," she instructed in a tone that indicated she would hear no argument. "And I'll thank you not to dawdle."

Mary Poppins marched ahead to take the lead. Georgie, amazed and delighted that their adventure had resulted in a nanny's magically appearing from the sky, hurried up to walk beside her.

The twins were not quite as delighted, however. They exchanged looks, sharing what they were thinking without having to speak, as twins will often do.

And what they were thinking was this: Who *was* this woman? Where had she come from? And why on earth did she think she could just show up and become their nanny?

CHAPTER 7

Michael and Jane were still in the attic, sorting through yet another box, when they heard Georgie call from the front door. "Father! Aunt Jane! Come quick!"

Michael raced to the attic stairs and climbed down. He hoped nothing had happened to any of the children. Had one of them tripped and hurt themselves? Why had he let them go to the grocer's alone? Once again, Michael was hit with a pang of longing for Kate. She never would have allowed something horrible like this to happen—whatever *this* was.

When Michael reached the second-floor landing, however, he looked down to find Georgie at the base of the stairs with a kite in his hand and a big smile on his face. "I was flying a kite and it got caught on a nanny!" Georgie shouted, waving the kite.

"Whatever are you talking about?" asked Jane, who had appeared behind Michael.

"Come and see!" Georgie said. He gestured toward the open front door.

Michael hurried down the stairs, followed by Jane. When they reached the floor, Michael got a closer look at the kite. "Where did you get that?" he asked Georgie.

"I found it in the park." Georgie pointed out the front door. "*She* kept it from blowing away."

Michael and Jane glanced toward the open doorway—and then gasped in disbelief as Mary Poppins stepped inside.

"Mary . . ." Michael began.

"Poppins?" Jane finished.

Mary Poppins shook her head sternly. "Close your mouth, please, Michael," she said. "We are *still* not a codfish."

Jane giggled. Mary Poppins cast her eyes toward

Jane. "Jane Banks—still rather inclined to giggle, I see."

Jane clapped a hand over her mouth. There was no doubt: this woman was the one and only *Mary Poppins*.

Annabel and John, out of breath, hurried up the front steps behind Mary Poppins. They were ready to explain to their father that the arrival of this strange woman at their house wasn't *their* idea. They had no idea who she was, or how she knew so much about them. Or why she had insisted on accompanying them home.

But before they could speak, they noticed their father and aunt staring at the woman with a different kind of surprise than the twins had felt. Their father and Aunt Jane, like Jack, seemed to actually *know* this prim and proper stranger.

"My heavens, it really *is* you!" Michael said to Mary Poppins. "You seem not to have aged in the slightest."

Mary Poppins shook her head in disapproval. "Really! How rude. One never discusses a woman's age, Michael. I would have hoped I had taught you better."

"I'm sorry," Michael said quickly. "I didn't mean . . ."

Jane rushed over to Mary Poppins and took hold of her arm. "I didn't think we'd ever see you again," she said, her face bright with delight. She had been about the same age as the twins when Mary Poppins had first come to their home. Mary Poppins had arrived on a windy day like this one. And her stay had been brief but memorable.

"It *is* wonderful to see you," Michael said sincerely. He turned to the children. "Mary Poppins used to be our nanny."

"What brings you here after all this time?" Jane asked Mary Poppins.

Mary Poppins set down her carpetbag and gazed around fondly at the familiar stairs and walls. "The same thing that brought me the first time," she said. "I've come to look after the Banks children."

Annabel and John exchanged looks. "Us?" Annabel asked. She folded her arms. "We don't need a nanny," she told Mary Poppins. "Mother taught us to take care of ourselves."

"You *did* just misplace Georgie," Mary Poppins pointed out.

"Only slightly," John protested. "We got him back."

"We can do anything a nanny can," Annabel insisted.

Georgie wasn't about to let his brother and sister chase Mary Poppins away. Not when she'd just soared down from the clouds especially for them. "Mary Poppins flew here on a kite," Georgie said to Annabel. "You can't do *that*, can you?"

"Don't be silly, Georgie," Michael said.

Jane smiled, remembering how whenever Mary Poppins was around, fanciful notions tended to pop into her head. "Oh, let him believe what he likes," she told Michael. She leaned down to Georgie. "When your father and I were young, we used to imagine Mary Poppins could do all sorts of impossible things."

Georgie wasn't listening, however. He'd noticed that the carved parrot head on the handle of Mary Poppins's umbrella had popped open its eyes. "*Actually . . .*" the parrot squawked.

"'Actually' what?" Michael asked, thinking Mary Poppins had spoken and not the umbrella.

Mary Poppins quickly pinched the parrot's beak shut before it could continue. "*Actually,*" she said, "I'd like to get back to the matter of my employment."

"Your umbrella talks!" Georgie exclaimed, pointing at its parrot head.

"Georgie, please," Michael said. "We're in the midst of a grown-up conversation."

Annabel took Georgie's hand. "Why don't we go up to the nursery?"

"But it *did* talk!" Georgie protested as Annabel and John led him upstairs. "I promise!"

After the children were out of sight, Michael turned back to Mary Poppins. "I'm afraid Georgie suffers from an excess of imagination at times," Michael said.

"As I recall, you had the same affliction yourself when you were young," Mary Poppins replied.

"Did I, really?" Michael's own childhood seemed, in his mind, to have taken place such a long time ago that he could barely even remember it. "Well, those days are long behind me."

Mary Poppins studied Michael a moment. "Are they, indeed?" she said. She nodded to herself, as if coming to a decision. "About my employment, then . . ."

"Yes, about that," Michael said. "The truth is I simply can't afford—"

"We can settle on terms later," Mary Poppins said, interrupting him. "I'll want my old room back, however, as long as it's not a complete disaster. And I insist on having every second Tuesday off."

Michael shook his head. The conversation was

getting out of his control. Mary Poppins had a way of getting directly to her point. That much he *did* remember from his childhood. "I'm afraid—"

"Of course, Mary Poppins," Jane said before Michael could finish. Michael shot Jane a bewildered look, which she ignored.

"That's all settled, then," Mary Poppins said. "Now, if you'll excuse me, the children have turned themselves into dustbins, and my first order of business is to see them properly bathed and dressed."

Michael realized it was futile to protest further, at least at the moment. He nodded and took Jane's arm, leading her into the parlor.

Once Jane and Michael were out of sight, Mary Poppins hopped onto the banister—and then glided up, as if by magic, leaving her carpetbag and umbrella behind. She hopped off at the top of the stairs just as Ellen exited one of the rooms, carrying an armful of fresh towels.

"Oh, hello, Mary Poppins," Ellen said, as if there was nothing strange about a woman sliding up a banister. And indeed there wasn't—not to Ellen. Ellen had worked for the Banks family from the time Jane and Michael were babies, and although there *were* a few things she tended to forget these days, she remembered Mary Poppins's visit very well. The housekeeper had always believed it was only a matter of time before the nanny returned.

Mary Poppins nodded hello and made her way to her old room at the end of the second-floor hallway.

Meanwhile, in the parlor, Michael drew Jane toward the mantel, far enough away from the front entrance hall that he could be sure Mary Poppins wouldn't hear them. "Have you gone mad?" he asked his sister. "I can't afford to take on anyone else."

"Mary Poppins isn't just anyone," Jane replied. "No one's hiring nannies anymore. The poor woman has no place to go."

"I might not, either, come the end of the week," Michael said, glancing down at the repossession notice, which he'd left on the desk.

Jane gave her brother a quick hug. "Don't be so grumpy," she told him. "You sound just like Father."

Michael pulled away, offended. "I do not!" Their father had been a wonderful man, but he'd had a tendency to be grouchy most of the time. Michael never wanted his children to think of *him* that way.

Jane patted Michael on the arm. "Give Mary Poppins a chance," she said. "You need help as much as she does."

"Very well," Michael said with a sigh. He knew Jane wouldn't give up until he agreed. "She can stay for the time being." He met Jane's eyes with a wry smile. "After all, she *did* fly all this way on a kite." They both laughed.

Jane paused a moment. "Those things, when we were young . . . they didn't really—"

"Happen?" Michael asked with a teasing note in his voice.

"Of course not," Jane said quickly.

"Ridiculous," Michael agreed. They laughed again.

At the same time, in the front entrance hallway—unseen by Michael or Jane—Mary Poppins had just slid up the banister. But that wasn't all: her parrot umbrella then rose and spun upside down, catching the handle of the carpetbag in its beak. The umbrella popped open and flew up the stairs with the bag.

"Why didn't Father believe you flew here on a kite?" Georgie asked Mary Poppins as she hung her coat and hat on a coatrack in the corner of the nanny's room.

"Because it's complete nonsense, of course," Mary Poppins replied. As she spoke, the parrot umbrella sailed into the room, carrying the carpetbag.

"Grown-ups forget," the parrot handle squawked, dropping the bag. "They always do."

Mary Poppins snatched the umbrella out of the air and gave the parrot a sharp look. "That will be quite enough of that," she told the parrot. "I should have left *you* in the umbrella stand." She closed the umbrella and leaned it in a corner. Mary Poppins then shooed Georgie through the adjoining bathroom and into the nursery, where John and Annabel were in hushed conversation on the far side of the room.

"What are you two whispering about?" Mary Poppins demanded.

The twins straightened up and faced her. "Nothing," they both said at the same time.

Mary Poppins regarded them dubiously. "Hmm. 'Nothing' is such a useful word, isn't it? It can mean anything and everything."

She crossed to the taller of the two wardrobes along the wall. She opened it and began rifling through the clothes hanging inside, looking for clean outfits for the children to change into.

Annabel stepped up beside her. "It's just that—"

"You don't require the services of a nanny," Mary Poppins interjected, having guessed what Annabel was going to say. She pulled out two sets of clothes and held them up in front of Annabel and John, who had joined his sister.

John peered over the top of the hanger. "We *have* grown up a good deal in the past year, after all," he said. Annabel nodded in agreement. They'd both had to take on a lot of responsibility since the death of their mother.

"We'll have to see what can be done about that," Mary Poppins replied as she handed the clothes to the twins. When she closed the wardrobe, she noticed the items on the nearby mantel were askew, and stepped over to straighten them out.

"That was our mother's," Annabel said as Mary Poppins reached for a china bowl. "Be careful."

Mary Poppins peered down at Annabel. "I am *always* careful."

"So . . . you're staying?" Annabel asked. It seemed pretty clear Mary Poppins could not be talked out of being their nanny.

"Yes, I'll stay," Mary Poppins replied. "Until the door opens."

"What does that mean?" asked John.

Annabel glanced at the door from the nursery to the hallway. Was that the door Mary Poppins meant? "That door is always opening," she told Mary Poppins. The door had warped over time and the latch no longer clicked into place. She closed the door to demonstrate, and it instantly bounced back open. "See?"

"Not that door," Mary Poppins said. "Another one." She moved to the smaller wardrobe and picked out an outfit for Georgie.

"The bathroom door?" Georgie asked, pointing to the door leading to the children's bathroom.

"That's just silly, Georgie," John told his brother. He turned to Mary Poppins, suddenly unsure. "Not the bathroom door?"

"No," Mary Poppins replied. "But a bath *would* prove useful." She took the clothes back from the twins and laid the outfits on the beds. "Come along," she told the children as she ushered them into the bathroom. "Time for a good, clean start."

"Our mother always had us take our baths in the evening," Annabel protested. Daylight streamed in through the green stained glass window above the white tub. It was barely noon. They hadn't even had lunch yet!

"In my experience, the perfect time of day to have a bath is when one needs a wash," Mary Poppins said. She instructed the children to strip down to their long underwear as she filled the bath with steaming hot water. She then gathered towels and washcloths from the shelves across the room and set them on a stool next to the tub. "Georgie will go in first," she said.

"We're perfectly capable of taking our own baths," John told the nanny, hoping she would leave them to bathe in peace. He and Annabel were used to taking charge—and Mary Poppins was getting in the way.

"How very helpful, John," Mary Poppins said. "In that case, you may turn off the tap." John reached out to follow her instruction, but Mary Poppins held up her hand. "Not quite yet," she said. "We still have to put in the bubbles." She stepped into her bedroom.

"But I don't like soap bubbles," John called after her.

"Then you shall have to try to avoid them at all costs," Mary Poppins replied as she returned with her carpetbag.

"All right," Annabel said with a sigh. It seemed there was no getting out of taking a bath. "But we'll have to be quick about it."

John nodded. "We still have to get to the grocer's," he said. He glanced at the window, which had darkened slightly and no longer had streaks of sunlight coming in, suggesting a storm might be coming. "Before it rains."

"I know who you should ask if it's going to rain," Georgie told John. He nodded toward the parrot umbrella in Mary Poppins's room. It was still leaning against the wall.

"Her umbrella can't talk, Georgie," Annabel told her brother.

Mary Poppins sniffed in disbelief, agreeing with Annabel. "The very idea," she said.

"How do you know it can't?" Georgie said. He'd seen the parrot talk! *Twice!* It was upsetting that no one seemed to believe him—even Mary Poppins, who had seen it herself.

"Because it can't," Annabel said firmly. "The idea of an umbrella talking is ridiculous."

Mary Poppins nodded. "Exactly right, Annabel. It's complete nonsense. Foolishness." She drew a bottle of soap bubbles from her bag.

"A talking umbrella makes no sense," John explained to Georgie. "And if it makes no sense, it can't be true."

"Quite right, John." Mary Poppins poured the soap bubbles into the steaming water, and frothy bubbles soon covered its surface. "Ridiculous things are ridiculous, and you children are *much* too grown-up to give in to imagination." A dolphin suddenly poked its head up through the bubbles. Mary Poppins tapped it on its snout. "Not yet," she whispered. The dolphin ducked back down under the bubbles.

John and Annabel stared in shock. Had they really seen that? A dolphin? Not a bath toy, but a full-size real live *dolphin?*

Georgie, however, wasn't shocked at all. He smiled at Mary Poppins. He had a feeling this was going to be the best bath he'd ever had.

"I'm also sure you are both too old to splash and play in the tub," Mary Poppins continued. She reached into her bag again and pulled out a pail—which was nearly the size of the bag—and a shovel, which was *much* bigger. John blinked. How was that possible? He turned to Annabel, who shrugged.

Mary Poppins dropped the items into the water and they quickly sank, disappearing from sight. She lifted a rubber duck from the bag and dropped it in as well. It, too, vanished.

"Too much imagination, too much mischief, too much wonder," Mary Poppins said as she produced a toy pirate ship from her bag and tossed it into the steaming water. "These are the types of things that are *much* too silly for serious children like you." She reached into her bag one more time and rooted around. She leaned down, reaching deeper and deeper, until her arm had disappeared up to her shoulder. "Ah!" she said finally. She smiled and drew her arm from the bag, opening her hand to reveal a palmful of shiny coins. She dropped them into the water one by one.

Mary Poppins peered into her now empty bag, a slight frown forming on her face. She glanced around the room and then snapped her fingers as if a thought had suddenly occurred to her. She quickly crossed to the sink and reached in. When she straightened up, she was holding a large beach umbrella. She returned to the tub and dropped it in.

Annabel and John watched the umbrella disappear. The twins then gaped in awe as the bubbles in the bath began to change color, from violet to orange to blue. It was becoming more and more difficult to figure out which was the strangest thing that had happened that day—because new, wondrous things *kept* occurring.

Mary Poppins folded her arms and studied the children a moment. "On second thought, perhaps you're right," she said. "It makes no sense to have a bath this early."

"But I *want* to take a bath!" Georgie protested. What he *really* wanted was to find that toy pirate ship and play with it.

"Really?" Mary Poppins said, sounding surprised. "Very well, then. Up you go!" She grabbed Georgie around the waist and lifted him onto the side of the tub. "And *in* you go." She nodded and he slid down the side of the tub into the water. Within seconds he'd vanished under the bubbles like the other objects.

"Georgie!" John reached into the water and grabbed Georgie's hand—but as he did, he felt a sharp tug and was pulled into the water himself. Soon he, too, had disappeared under the bubbles.

"John!" Annabel shouted. She leaned over and batted away the bubbles, trying to see into the water. "Georgie!" But there was no sign of her brothers or any of the things Mary Poppins had dropped into the tub. "What happened?" she asked Mary Poppins. "Will they be all right?"

Mary Poppins shrugged. "It's just a bath, after all." She thought a minute. "But then again, it's not my tub."

"Shouldn't you go after them?" Annabel said. What kind of nanny lets the children in her care vanish down a drain?

Mary Poppins shook her head. "I had my bath this morning, thank you," she told Annabel.

"If you won't, I will!" Annabel climbed over the side of the tub and slid into the water. Within seconds she had vanished under the bubbles like her brothers.

Mary Poppins glanced around the empty room. "Oh, well," she sighed. "I suppose I should." She perched herself on the edge of the tub, then slid in backwards, kicking her legs up as they submerged into the bubbles.

Then Mary Poppins, like the children, disappeared.

CHAPTER
9

Georgie and the twins tumbled through the blue-green water, their bodies spinning wildly as they sank deeper and deeper into this mysterious sea. Georgie grinned as he twirled about, but Annabel and John kept trying to turn themselves right side up. That was impossible, however, because they were sinking too fast—and who was to say what *was* right side up, anyway, since there was nothing to see in any direction but water?

Annabel noticed they no longer were wearing the long underwear they'd had on in the bathroom before sliding into the tub. Instead they were now in matching blue-and-white striped bathing suits with short sleeves and pants that went to the knees. Mary Poppins appeared above them, dressed in a similar bathing suit. She waved to Annabel as she floated past.

After a few moments, Annabel saw they were nearing the bottom of the ocean. Schools of colorful fish swirled around them as their bare feet touched down onto the soft sand. Nearby, pretty coral reefs swayed to and fro.

The toys Mary Poppins had dropped into the bath had also landed in the sand—and had all grown to enormous sizes. The rubber duck was now as big as a bus, and the pail and shovel tossed in with it towered above it. The toy pirate ship had become a full-size shipwreck. Georgie's eyes opened wide in amazement and delight.

As the children swam around the gigantic objects, they spotted people they knew from Cherry Tree Lane, going about their business as if they were still on land. One neighbor was pinning shirts to a clothesline.

"Clothes drying at the bottom of the sea?" Mary Poppins declared to the children. "Ludicrous!"

Willoughby suddenly dog-paddled past, towing Miss Lark behind him on his leash. "Dogs paddling on a leash underwater?" Mary Poppins continued. "Impossible!"

What was just as impossible was that Mary Poppins's words didn't sound as if they were being spoken under-water. There were no bubbles and they didn't sound gurgled. Her voice was as loud and clear as it was when she was on land.

The milkman appeared on the deck of the pirate ship, passing milk bottles to a family of catfish. "A milk-man on a pirate ship?" Mary Poppins said. "Nonsensical!"

Georgie dove through a patch of thick seagrass toward the pirate ship, passing the park-keeper from their neighborhood park, who pointed sternly to a sign that read KEEP OFF THE SEAGRASS. Georgie frowned. It seemed even in the ocean there were bothersome rules to follow. He paddled over to John, who had already reached the deck of the ship. John had a rusted sundial in his hands and was angling it this way and that, try-ing to tell the time, but they were too far underwater for the sun to reach them.

A few feet away, Annabel peered into one of the pirate ship's portholes and was amazed when she saw Ellen inside, stirring a pot of soup on a stove—and trying to stop the clams and minnows she was cooking from swim-ming away. Mary Poppins glided up next to Annabel and whispered in her ear: "Seafood chowder cooked under the sea? Preposterous!" Mary Poppins smiled and spun around, gesturing for Annabel to follow her.

Annabel waved to her brothers as she swam past, and the boys paddled over to join her. Mary Poppins led the children around the side of the ship to a treasure chest, perched on a reef. The chest was filled with coins like those Mary Poppins had dropped into the bathtub, but now there were hundreds of them, perhaps even thousands.

"Imagine!" Mary Poppins said, tossing the coins into the water around them. "Pirates' treasure? It's just too silly."

Mary Poppins broke off three sponges from the reef and tossed them to the children. "Be sure to scrub behind your ears!" she said. She then signaled to a school of dolphins, which swam toward them and circled the children, creating a whirlpool of bubbles.

The water was so warm and the bubbles were so soft that John ceased to care what time it was. He stopped worrying about where they were or how they got there. And so did Annabel. Like Georgie, the twins finally started to *enjoy* themselves.

When the bubbles cleared, all three children were thoroughly scrubbed and washed—but they were also trapped inside enormous bubbles, which carried them upward, with Mary Poppins swimming alongside. The bubbles reached the surface—but then kept going. Annabel, John, and Georgie soon found themselves floating above the water, still encased in their clear soapy globes. Annabel peered out through the bubble. The ocean seemed to go forever in each direction, with no sign of land anywhere; the sky above was a deep, clear blue, without a cloud in sight.

Annabel glanced down to see Mary Poppins seated inside their tub, which was floating on the water like a boat.

Mary Poppins reached for something at her feet and straightened up, now holding the beach umbrella. She used its tip to pop Annabel's bubble, and Annabel dropped into the tub. Mary Poppins then popped John's and Georgie's bubbles as well, and they fell into the tub next to Annabel.

Mary Poppins opened the umbrella and handed it to John. "An umbrella for a sail," she said with a laugh. "How ridiculous. How silly. How *un*imaginable." As she said this, the umbrella caught the wind, propelling the tub across the surface of the ocean.

As the tub sped forward, the wind and the warm sun dried the children's hair and bathing suits. They felt cleaner than they'd ever felt in their whole lives.

Another boat appeared up ahead. It was a small rowboat, and inside sat Admiral Boom and First Mate Binnacle. "Ahoy!" Admiral Boom called out to the group. The two men saluted Mary Poppins and the three young sailors.

As the children saluted back, John lost his balance. The umbrella/sail tipped to one side and John fell, plopping into the water. He lost hold of the umbrella, which floated away.

"Man overboard!" Admiral Boom shouted.

Mary Poppins and Annabel reached over the side of the tub and grabbed John's arms. They hauled him into the tub, and he landed with a soggy *splat*, his bathing suit once again drenched. John shook off the water, looking a little like Willoughby after a rainstorm. His damp hair poked up from his head in erratic points.

Annabel and Georgie laughed. John pouted a

moment, but his sour mood didn't last, and within seconds, he had joined in on the laughter.

Mary Poppins smiled. "Perhaps the impossible *can* be possible now and then," she said. "And the silly and the ridiculous can be fun."

"Yes!" Georgie declared. Annabel and John exchanged looks and nodded. Their brother was right. It had been so long since they'd had that much fun. They'd almost forgotten what having fun was like, but Mary Poppins had reminded them.

Mary Poppins was satisfied the bath had served its purpose. She reached down and pulled the chain attached to the bathtub plug. Water immediately rushed up through the drain, filling the tub and creating a whirlpool that caused the tub to spin, faster and faster. The whirlpool grew bigger, and within seconds the tub was sucked down into it, disappearing under the surface.

Everything went dark for a moment—and then the children found themselves once again in their bathroom, standing next to the tub, wrapped in towels. They watched the water swirl down the drain inside the tub. When the water was gone, all that remained was the tiny toy pirate ship, leaning to one side against the damp porcelain.

The children quickly got dressed and raced downstairs to tell their father and Aunt Jane about their adventure. They found Michael and Jane in the parlor, which was a complete mess, with books and papers scattered everywhere. After searching the attic for the bank shares certificate—with no luck—the adults had returned to search the first floor.

Jane sat at the secretary's desk, sifting through the papers inside. Michael stood in front of an empty bookshelf, flipping through the pages of a book, hoping to find the certificate stuck inside. The books he'd already searched lay in messy piles at his feet.

"We went sailing!" Georgie shouted as he dashed into the room. He ran up to his father and hugged him, causing Michael to drop the book.

"Not now, please," Michael said sharply. He was beginning to fear that the certificate was nowhere in the house, and he wasn't in the mood for Georgie's fanciful stories.

"But it really happened!" John insisted.

Annabel nodded. "It did!"

John turned to Mary Poppins who'd appeared in the doorway behind them. "Tell them, Mary Poppins!"

Mary Poppins smoothed a lock of her hair back into its bun. "I have no idea what you're all talking about," she said.

"We swam through a pirate ship," Georgie told his father. "And there was treasure, and then we floated up in the air in bubbles, and then—"

"Enough! Please!" Michael clapped his hands over his ears.

Georgie backed away, frightened by his father's anger. John and Annabel hurried to their brother's sides and wrapped their arms around him protectively.

"Michael!" Jane shook her head at her brother, disappointed he would take his frustrations out on his children.

"We're sorry, Father," Annabel said. The twins guided Georgie toward the stairs.

"No, wait," Michael said, rushing over to them. "*I'm* sorry." He knelt down and drew them close in a hug. "I don't mean to be cross with you. It's just that I've lost something very important."

"We'll find it," Jane said firmly. "I'm sure it was

simply tucked away somewhere for safekeeping."

As soon as Jane said this, Michael realized exactly where the certificate had to be. "The bank!" he said. "Didn't Father have a safety-deposit box?"

"Yes, of course he did!" Jane said. She clasped her hands together in happiness and relief. "We'll go first thing in the morning."

Michael's smile faded. "What about the key?" he said. They'd need the key to open the box.

"I saw a box of keys in Father's wardrobe," Jane told him.

Michael gave his children another hug. "Everything's all right now," he assured them. "You mind Mary Poppins. Your aunt and I will see you later." He and Jane then hurried out of the room.

Mary Poppins scowled at the mess the adults had left behind. "My goodness, gracious, glory me!" she said. "You'd think by now they'd have learned to pick up after themselves." She plucked a piece of paper off the floor and carried it to a wastebasket. The second after she dropped it in, the other papers on the floor magically rose into the air. The children watched in awe as the papers swirled around the room, collecting themselves together into a neat pile before they all dropped into the basket on their own.

Mary Poppins faced the children and folded her arms. "Cleaning is not a spectator sport," she scolded. "John, Annabel, put all the books back on the shelves." She handed the wastebasket to Georgie. "Georgie, I want you to take this out to the rubbish."

Georgie carried the wastebasket through the dining room and the kitchen and then out the back door to the alley. He tipped the contents into the rubbish bin, but one of the pieces of paper floated back up to him. He snatched it out of the air.

Georgie set down the basket and studied the paper. It was one of Michael's old drawings, a sketch of their house with the family standing out front. Michael had his arms around John and Annabel, and next to them stood the children's mother, beautiful and smiling, holding the baby Georgie in her arms.

It was clear to Georgie that the drawing didn't want to be thrown out. It had flown up to him for a reason. He didn't know what the reason was yet, but he would keep the sketch until he found out. He folded it up and put it in his pocket.

CHAPTER
10

The storm that had seemed to be coming finally arrived the next morning. A sea of black umbrellas flowed through the streets of London, and hundreds of rain boots sloshed over the city's wet cobblestones.

At the Fidelity Fiduciary Bank, torrents of rain cascaded down in front of the building's grand entrance. It pounded the pavement as people marched past, clutching their umbrellas, huddled against the cold and wet weather. Those inside the bank could hear the rain relentlessly battering the windows.

Deep inside the bank's vault, however, Michael heard nothing but the faint rustling of papers as he sifted through the family's safety-deposit box. The bank officer stood a polite distance away.

Michael dropped the papers back into the box and looked over at Jane, who was waiting across from him expectantly. He shook his head sadly. The box held only family documents, like the children's birth certificates and the deed to the house—the house they were on the verge of losing. The bank shares certificate was not inside.

"That's that," Michael told his sister. He gestured for the bank officer to take the box and lock it up again.

"What about Mr. Dawes, Jr.?" Jane asked. "Couldn't he give you more time?" Mr. Dawes, Jr., had been the bank president from the time Jane and Michael were children.

"I'm sure he would if he were still here," Michael told Jane. "Dawes's nephew Mr. Wilkins has been running things lately and I'm not even sure he knows who I am."

"Well, it's high time he finds out, don't you think?" Jane said. Before Michael could respond, Jane marched out the bank vault door and into the lobby.

Michael hurried after her. "Jane!" he called out.

"Where are you going?" His words echoed against the lobby's marble floor and walls. Customers glanced over at him curiously.

Jane had already reached the staircase at the far end of the lobby. Michael rushed after her. "Jane!" he whispered loudly. But Jane either didn't hear him or was ignoring him, because she continued up the steps without breaking her stride.

Michael darted up the stairs after her. He hurried down the hallway, reaching Jane just as she arrived outside Mr. Wilkins's office, and grabbed her arm as he paused to catch his breath. "We can't just walk into his office," he said finally, once somewhat composed.

The door to Mr. Wilkins's outer office was open, which seemed to Jane like an obvious invitation to come in. She gently pulled free of Michael's grip and entered.

Jane glanced around the space, remembering when she and Michael would come to the bank when they were children. Not much had changed, except for the secretary. The old one must have retired. Now sitting behind the desk was a pretty young woman with short wavy hair, who glanced up at Jane curiously. The plaque in front of the secretary read MISS PENNY FARTHING.

"Good morning, Miss Farthing," Jane said.

"Good morning," Miss Farthing replied warily.

Michael stepped in and reached for Jane's arm, but she stepped to the side, evading his grasp. "Remember how the old secretary always had that jar of sweets on her desk?" she asked him.

Before Michael could reply, a gentleman emerged from the doorway behind Miss Farthing. "*I* remember them," he said. He was a handsome older man with a thin mustache and a kind smile. "Those little toffees that stuck your teeth together." He turned to the secretary. "We should get you one of those jars, Miss Farthing."

"Of course, sir," Miss Farthing replied with a nod.

The gentleman crossed over to Jane and Michael. "This wouldn't happen to be your sister, would it, Mr. Banks?" he asked Michael.

Michael was too surprised by the fact that Mr. Wilkins knew his name to respond. Jane quickly held out her hand. "Yes," she said. "I'm Jane Banks. How do you do?"

Mr. Wilkins shook her hand. "William Weatherall Wilkins," he said, introducing himself. "It's a pleasure to meet you, Miss Banks." He gestured for Michael and Jane to accompany him into his office. Jane smiled at Michael as they followed Mr. Wilkins in. She felt sure this kind man would help them solve their problem.

Mr. Wilkins waved to the two chairs in front of his desk, gesturing for Jane and Michael to sit. "What can I do for you today?" he asked as he sat down opposite them. Behind his desk, light raindrops gently beat against a giant window, which was framed by long velvet curtains with gold trim. The rain had let up, affording those facing the window a view of Big Ben in the distance. Opposite the window, behind Michael and Jane, was a fireplace, with a roaring fire that filled the room with warmth.

Michael handed Mr. Wilkins the notice Mr. Gooding and Mr. Frye had brought to the house the day before. He explained how he'd taken out a loan with the bank and had fallen behind on payments.

Mr. Wilkins studied the notice. "If I'd known George Banks's son had taken out a loan with us, I'd have handled the paperwork myself," he said. But then he returned the notice to Michael. "Unfortunately, at this point, there's very little I can do."

"Our father did leave us shares in the bank," Michael said.

Mr. Wilkins blinked in surprise. "Oh, well, that *is* good news," he said with an encouraging smile.

"The problem is we can't seem to find the shares certificate," Jane explained.

"You wouldn't happen to have any record of our father's shares?" Michael asked.

"Yes, indeed," Mr. Wilkins replied with a nod. "I would think so." He pressed a button on his intercom. "Would you bring in the shareholder's ledger, Miss Farthing?" he said into the box.

Miss Farthing's voice came from the speaker: "Right away, Mr. Wilkins."

"What about your uncle, Mr. Dawes, Jr.?" Jane asked Mr. Wilkins. "He would know if our father received shares, wouldn't he?"

Mr. Wilkins gazed at the portrait of his uncle hanging above the fireplace and shook his head with a sigh. "I'm afraid dear old Uncle Dawes is getting on in years." He tapped his index finger to his temple. "*Non compos mentis*," he whispered. "Which, sadly, is why I had to take over for him."

Jane knew *"Non compos mentis"* was Latin for "not in one's right mind." She was sorry to hear this. She remembered Mr. Dawes, Jr., being one of the sharpest and most quick-witted people she had ever met. But then she thought of Ellen and Admiral Boom. Both were still in their right minds, but those minds had definitely slowed down a little over the past several years.

Miss Farthing entered the room, carrying a large rectangular book. "Thank you, Miss Farthing," Mr. Wilkins said as he took the ledger and placed it on his desk. He flipped it open, revealing lined pages filled with names and dates. He paged through to the *B*s and then ran his index finger down a column. "Let's see," he murmured. "Babcock, Baker . . . hmm. There's no listing for George Banks here." He closed the ledger and stood up. "Don't despair," he told the siblings, giving them another warm, encouraging smile. "You have until that big fellow out there chimes his last on Friday night to find that certificate." He gestured out the window toward Big Ben. "I'll keep searching here as well."

"Thank you so much, Mr. Wilkins," Michael said, reaching out to shake the bank president's hand.

Jane did the same. "Yes, thank you," she said. "It was such a pleasure to meet you."

Mr. Wilkins continued to smile as he moved around his desk and led Jane and Michael to the door. Once he had closed the door behind them, however, his smile faded. He returned to his desk and reopened the ledger, then pressed the button on his intercom. "Bring me all of George Banks's old files, would you?" he said.

"Of course, Mr. Wilkins," Miss Farthing replied.

Mr. Wilkins ran his finger down the ledger's page, as he had before, but this time his finger stopped on a name: GEORGE BANKS. Mr. Wilkins smiled, but it wasn't a kind, warm, or encouraging smile. It was a cold, cruel, conniving one. He then took the corner of the page between his thumb and forefinger and yanked it, ripping the page completely out.

Mr. Wilkins crumpled the page into a ball and tossed it into the fireplace. The paper burst into flames, and within moments, it had turned to ash.

CHAPTER
11

The rain had ended by that evening, and a misty dusk settled over the London streets. Up in the Bankses' nursery, the children had changed into their pajamas, though it was not quite bedtime. Annabel was putting away the children's clean clothes in the wardrobes, and Mary Poppins had sent John downstairs to help Ellen clean the dishes, because in addition to her forgetfulness, Ellen had a tendency to drop things.

Georgie, having not been given a chore to do, had devoted himself to the important work of jumping up and down on his bed as if it was a trampoline. Mary

Poppins glanced over at him as she entered the room and crossed to the windows to draw the curtains. "This is a nursery, let me remind you, Georgie, not a music hall," she told him.

"Can we have another bath?" Georgie asked, still bouncing.

"Oh, pishposh," Mary Poppins said dismissively. She noticed the broken kite leaning against Georgie's bed. "And if you're hoping I'll let you take this sadly neglected kite to the park tomorrow, you had better start patching it up this instant." She moved to the window that looked down to the street, and waved to Jack, who was polishing one of the brass lamps on the front portico of the house.

Georgie, thrilled at the idea of another exciting kite-flying adventure, hopped off the bed. He picked up the kite and examined the rips. He'd need paper to patch them up; he then remembered the sketch he'd taken out of the rubbish. He'd placed the sketch under his pillow, but he pulled it out now and unfolded it. It would be a shame to rip it up, but he would make sure to tear around the image of the family so that portion would remain intact. It even felt right to use the drawing, somehow. The kite had already brought a nanny to their house! Who knew what other magic it could perform?

Meanwhile, Jack swung himself up onto the portico roof and climbed along the ledge to the balcony outside the nursery window. Since it wasn't too late, it seemed like a nice time to have a chat. He gave Annabel and Georgie each a wave, and they waved back before returning to their tasks. "When I was a lad, I used to wave up to the boy and girl who lived here," he told Mary Poppins as he took a seat on the windowsill.

"You mean Michael and Jane," Mary Poppins said.

Jack nodded. "Miss Jane Banks, that's right. I see Mr. Banks now and again, but it's been ages since I've seen her."

"She lives in a flat on the other side of town now," Mary Poppins told Jack. "I'm sure you'll bump into her one of these days."

"Course, we all heard about Mr. Banks's wife," Jack said quietly. "I know what that's like, losing your parents so young." He nodded toward the children. "It's a good thing you came along when you did, Mary Poppins."

Mary Poppins gazed over at Georgie, who was carefully patching the kite. "Indeed," she said to herself.

Downstairs, Ellen handed the clean dinner plates to John, who stood on a chair in front of the china cabinet.

"You're such a 'elp, you are," Ellen told him. "I only wish I could do somethin' to 'elp your father save this old house." She thought a minute. "I could sell my brooch and necklace, I suppose. A matching set, it is. Me mum gave 'em to me."

John looked down at Ellen, touched by her generosity. "You'd do that for us?" he asked.

Ellen leaned toward him and winked. "I think they're fakes anyway," she whispered. She picked up a large serving bowl from the dining table and lifted it up to him. "There's plenty in this house worth more than my old trinkets."

John stared down at the serving bowl. Of course! He should have thought of it earlier! "Excuse me," he said, jumping off the chair and dashing out of the room before Ellen could reply. He raced through the parlor and leapt up the stairs two by two. He couldn't wait to tell Annabel his idea.

Inside the nursery, Georgie was taping ripped pieces of the sketch onto the kite while Annabel sat in bed, reading a book. Mary Poppins was still at the window, talking to Jack.

John burst into the room and hurried over to Annabel. He took her hand, pulling her out of bed. "I know how to save the house," he told her in an urgent whisper.

"What do you mean?" Annabel asked.

Mary Poppins glanced over her shoulder at the twins. "If you two are going to keep up all this whispering, I would like you to practice doing so as loudly as possible," she said. "It will still be bad manners, but at least then we'll all be in on the secret."

John ignored her and drew Annabel over to the mantel. He took down the china bowl Mary Poppins had adjusted the day before.

"What are you doing?" Annabel said under her breath. "We're not supposed to touch that."

"This is authentic china, Annabel," John told her. He held it up. An illustration had been delicately painted on the side. It was of a coachman steering a horse and empty carriage along a winding tree-lined path. The illustration continued inside the bowl, showing the path leading to a park where a handsomely dressed couple strolled toward a stone arch.

"Mother always said it was priceless," John continued. "If we sold it, I bet it'd be enough to pay off Father's debt."

Annabel grabbed the bowl from John. "That's a terrible idea. Mother loved that bowl."

John grabbed it back. "But she'd sell it herself to save the house," he insisted.

Georgie saw John and Annabel fighting over the bowl and rushed over to them, forgetting about the kite. "That was Mother's," he told John. "Put it back." He reached for the bowl. Soon all three were fighting over the bowl. They yanked it from side to side, this way and that, until the bowl suddenly slipped from their grasp and fell to the floor—*SMASH!*—cracking, with a wedge-shaped piece breaking off from the rim.

"That didn't sound good, did it?" Jack whispered to

Mary Poppins. She frowned and marched over to the children.

"Give me the missing piece," John whispered to Annabel as Mary Poppins approached.

"I haven't got it," she said. Annabel glanced around the floor for the broken wedge while John quickly set the bowl back on the mantelpiece and turned it to hide the cracked side.

"Which of you broke the bowl?" Mary Poppins demanded. Before they could protest, she opened her hand, which held the missing piece.

"Georgie did," John said, pointing to his brother.

"I did not!" Georgie protested. "It was Annabel."

"John was the one who took it down from the mantel," Annabel said.

"Actually, it was all three of them," announced a mysterious male voice with a heavy Cockney accent.

"Who said that?" John asked. The children glanced around, confused. Who had spoken? It wasn't Jack, who was still on the other side of the room.

"Oh, dear," Mary Poppins said, glancing at the bowl.

The children followed her gaze and discovered the painted illustration had changed. The carriage was now tipped to the side, and one of its wheels lay nearby. The coachman was crouched down, peering at the empty axle, and the horse was staring out from the image—straight at the children. Even though the illustration was tiny, the horse's annoyed expression came through sharp and clear.

"It seems they've broken your carriage wheel," Mary Poppins said to the bowl.

"That they have," called out a different voice. This one had an Irish lilt to it, and it seemed to be coming from inside the bowl. "Wheel's useless now," the voice noted.

"Useless as a chocolate teapot," said the first voice.

"Who's going to fix that, then?" asked the second voice.

Jack crossed the room to join the others. "Them what broke it fixes it, I say," he said. "What do you think, Mary Poppins?"

Mary Poppins let out an irritated sigh. "I suppose we have no choice," she said.

The children stared at each other, now even more baffled. "How are we going to do *that*?" John asked.

"I know a bit about fixing carriages," Jack offered.

"We can't fix their carriage wheel," Annabel insisted, pointing to the illustration. "It's impossible!"

"Everything is possible," Mary Poppins told Annabel. "Even the impossible." She picked up the bowl and set it on a small table in the center of the nursery. She then gently pressed the missing piece back in place. "Gather around, everyone. Spit-spot." She waved to Jack and the children, who huddled close to her. "Ready?" she asked. The others nodded. Mary Poppins grabbed the bowl between her hands and gave it a spin.

The bowl turned, picking up speed, until the illustration was only a blur. The children watched in astonishment as colorful leaves burst up from inside the bowl and blew in all directions. The leaves filled the nursery, swirling around the group, until they were all the children could see. The air seemed to change. To Georgie, it smelled of fresh breezes and playgrounds, of autumn and cool evenings—of excitement and adventure.

CHAPTER
12

Georgie noticed they didn't tumble like they had when they'd slipped through the bathtub into the ocean. They didn't seem to be moving at all, in fact. Only the leaves were moving, but they gradually slowed to a flutter, floating down around the group. When the leaves completely fell away, Georgie and the others were standing on a tree-lined path.

John blinked. "What just happened?" he asked.

"Where are we?" Annabel queried, gazing around in wonder.

Jack lifted a finger and tapped the air. Each tap made a *tink tink* sound, as if he was tapping against porcelain.

"Looks like we're in *china*," he said. "So to speak."

And they were—actually *inside* the illustration on the side of the china bowl. They stood at the top of a hill, the part of the illustration near the bowl's lip. The carriage was parked below them, farther down the path.

If that wasn't surprising enough, they were all wearing turn-of-the-century clothing. Each outfit appeared as if it had been delicately painted, so they looked like they belonged in the world inside the bowl. Georgie, who was now holding Gillie, was dressed in a sailor suit, complete with a blue sailor's cap. John wore a plaid yellow suit with short pants and a jacket and had a straw hat on his head. Annabel's peach-colored dress matched her peach-colored hat, which had a peach ribbon down the back.

Jack's outfit was even more colorful. He looked a little like a circus ringmaster in his bright aquamarine top hat and jacket and his green-and-aquamarine-plaid vest and green-and-orange-striped trousers.

Mary Poppins was dressed the most elegantly of all, in a pink-and-white-striped skirt with a bustle in the back. Her hair was pinned up in a graceful swirl beneath a small oval hat on which sat two artificial birds: one pink and one blue. She wore fingerless gloves made of daintily embroidered lace and held a pink parasol in one hand.

To the children's shock and initial dismay, Mary Poppins sat down in her beautiful dress, right on the path they had landed on. "Come on, everyone!" she said. "That wheel won't fix itself." She pushed off, sliding down the porcelain slope and coming to a smooth stop beside the carriage, where she stood up and waved to the others to follow.

Georgie sat down, with Gillie on his lap, and pushed off, followed by Jack and the twins. "Tread lightly, please!" Mary Poppins called up to them. "This is fine porcelain. We don't want to chip the glaze."

Georgie lost his balance as he slid, and somersaulted past the carriage. "Head up and feet beneath you," Mary Poppins shouted to him. Georgie tumbled to a stop, landing on his back. When Annabel and John reached the carriage, they stood up and hurried over to help their brother.

Mary Poppins approached the coachman, who was still crouched down over the broken axle. "Excuse me, driver," she said.

When the coachman stood up and turned around, the children discovered he was an Irish setter! He stood on his hind legs and was as tall as a man. "Is that yourself, Mary Poppins?" the coachman said with a smile.

John pointed to the coachman. "He's . . ."

Annabel gaped. "You're . . ."

"That's right," the coachman said with a nod. "I'm Irish. Also part poodle." His was the second voice they'd heard coming from the bowl. John and Annabel exchanged glances. An Irish setter that drove a carriage—and talked!

Mary Poppins smiled, not at all surprised that a dog stood before her. "How wonderful to see you, Shamus," she said sincerely. "And Clyde as well, of course," she added, nodding toward the horse.

Georgie leaned over to Annabel. "She's talking to a dog!" he said in amazement.

Clyde turned his head and stared at the children. "Well, *of course* she can talk!" Clyde exclaimed in his Cockney accent. He shook his head. Children could be so silly at times.

The children's mouths widened further. They were even more bewildered. The horse was the other voice they'd heard coming from the bowl. What *was* this place they'd come to, where animals could speak?

Mary Poppins gestured to the broken wheel with her parasol. "So sorry about all this," she told Shamus. "If you would help Jack lift the carriage, the children will put the wheel back on."

"With pleasure!" Shamus replied.

Mary Poppins waved to the children to pick up the wheel. "Take your places, everyone," she said. Jack joined the coachman at the carriage. As Clyde watched over his shoulder, Jack and Shamus lifted the corner of the carriage, and the children carefully placed the wheel back onto the axle.

The bolt that had attached the wheel to the axle had rolled away, however. Mary Poppins glanced around for a replacement. She snapped her fingers as an idea came to her, and reached into her sleeve, removing a long scarf. "This should do it!" she said. She wrapped the scarf around the spokes and axle, tying the wheel in place. She then tugged on the ends of the scarf to tighten it. "There we are!" she said when she'd finished. She brushed off her hands. "Shipshape!"

Shamus studied the repaired wheel. "Not a bad job of it," he said, admiring her work.

Clyde, however, was not as impressed. Whoever heard of repairing a carriage wheel with a *scarf*? He shook his head and neighed in resignation, realizing there was no better solution. "S'pose it'll have to do," he said.

Mary Poppins turned to the children. "Back to the nursery," she said, waving them toward the hill.

"*Already?*" Annabel said. They'd only just begun their adventure. It didn't seem right to end it so soon.

John felt the same. "Can't we stay in the bowl for a *little* while longer?" he asked.

"I want a carriage ride!" Georgie insisted. He definitely didn't want to go back yet. What if they found another pirate ship—or something even *more* exciting?

Jack grinned at Mary Poppins. "I wouldn't mind a carriage ride m'self," he said.

Mary Poppins thought it over a moment. "I suppose it wouldn't do any harm," she said finally. "Would you mind?" she asked Shamus, who had returned to the driver's seat.

"Not at all," he replied, tipping his hat. He waved to

Jack and the children. "Climb aboard, everyone!"

The children shouted with glee. Jack helped them into the carriage, followed by Mary Poppins, and then hopped in himself.

"Where would you all like to go this fine day?" Shamus asked the group.

The children had no idea where they *were*, which made it difficult to decide where they wanted to *go*.

Mary Poppins, however, knew exactly where they were—and precisely where they should go. "The Music Hall, please," she told Shamus. Shamus nodded and tapped his whip on Clyde's flanks.

As Clyde trotted off down the path, John leaned over to Mary Poppins. "Where?" he asked, to be sure they'd heard correctly.

"We're on the brink of an adventure, John," Mary Poppins told him. "Don't spoil it with too many questions." She smiled. "You had a whole other world sitting on your mantel, and you never knew it."

Annabel gazed around as they traveled down the path, past a small pond and flowering shrubs. How could they have known the image on the bowl was actually a real place? Come to think of it, how could they have known there was an entire ocean down the drain of their bathtub?

The answer seemed to be that they *couldn't* have known—not until Mary Poppins had arrived to open their eyes to the unseen wonders of the world.

Shamus steered the carriage up the hill, around the outside of the bowl, heading for the top. When they reached the lip, Annabel could feel the carriage tipping sideways. "Hold on!" Jack called out, clutching the side of the carriage. The children quickly grabbed the side. They cried out as the carriage nearly flipped upside down crossing over the lip. Only Mary Poppins remained calm, holding lightly on to her hat, smiling as the carriage turned right side up again and carried them down into the bowl.

Jack the lamplighter gets ready to dim the streetlamp in front of the Bankses' home.

Jane Banks visits her brother, Michael, and his three children, John, Annabel, and Georgie.

Michael Banks has fallen behind on a loan he took out to pay bills after his wife passed away.

Mary Poppins floats down from the sky on the tail of Georgie's kite.

How does this mysterious woman who has just arrived by kite know the children's names?

Jane and Michael go to the bank to search for their bank shares certificate.

Mr. Wilkins, the bank president, tells Jane and Michael they have until midnight on Friday to find their bank shares certificate.

Bath time becomes an underwater adventure with Mary Poppins.

Mary Poppins brings an element of fun to everyday tasks, like cleaning the house.

A magical world awaits inside the china bowl.

The children tell Mary Poppins they miss their mother.

Jack offers everyone a ride on his bike.

The leeries do a bit of kick and prance in the park.

There's nowhere to go but up at the spring fair.

When the front door opens, Mary Poppins bids farewell to 17 Cherry Tree Lane.

CHAPTER

13

The tree-lined path continued, looking much the same as it had outside the bowl, but Annabel sensed there was a spark of something strange and unusual in the air inside the bowl. The flowers seemed twice as fragrant, and the colors seemed brighter and bolder.

"I should warn you things are very different in here," Mary Poppins told the children. She held out her hand, and a hummingbird with brilliant silver-blue wings landed on her finger. "This is a world where the animals entertain—and come to *be* entertained."

Ahead, a couple in fancy dress walked along one side

of the path. When the carriage reached them, the couple was revealed to be two doves. They nodded politely to the children as the carriage passed. Annabel and John smiled back and tried not to stare, knowing that would be rude.

The setting sun sent warm rays through the trees as a gang of monkeys swung from branch to branch. Georgie, eager to get a better view, climbed up to join Shamus in the driver's seat. Shamus took off his hat and offered it to Georgie with a wink. Georgie grinned and swapped his sailor's cap for the top hat. The coachman's hat was too big for him, and it slid down to his ears, but if he tipped it back, he would have a perfect view of whatever amazing thing they would certainly be coming across next. And sure enough, he soon spotted a real giraffe in a seersucker suit pedaling a penny-farthing bicycle. The vehicle's tall seat and huge front wheel were a perfect fit for the giraffe's long legs. Georgie held up Gillie to show him.

"Nearly there, Mary Poppins!" Shamus called out. A pair of elaborately designed gates appeared ahead, with the words "Music Hall" scrolled in the ironwork.

Jack leaned over to Annabel and John. "You'll see birds lining up to get inside," Jack told the twins.

"And penguins waiting behind the curtain," added Mary Poppins.

"You might see cats playing the fiddle and pigs acting like big hams," Jack said with a grin.

"It's quite a fantastical place," Mary Poppins told the children.

"Phantasmagorical," Jack added.

"Super-spectacular," Mary Poppins insisted.

"Marvelous!" Jack cried.

"Miraculous!" Mary Poppins countered.

"Impossible!" Jack declared.

Mary Poppins gave Jack a stern look. "Oh, no, Jack," she said. "Not impossible. Absurd and far-fetched, perhaps. But never impossible."

The carriage passed through gates, arriving in the middle of a large field. The children looked around. "Where's the Music Hall?" asked Annabel.

Mary Poppins laughed. "Oh, yes. Silly me," she said. She opened her parasol and twirled it above their heads. The pink-and-white fabric spun at a dizzying speed, and the parasol grew larger and larger, transforming itself into a giant music hall tent several yards away from the carriage.

Annabel, stunned, leaned over to Jack. "How did she do that?" she asked.

Jack shrugged. "One thing you should know about Mary Poppins is that she never explains *anything*."

The day had magically become nighttime. The top of the tent was festooned with strings of lights that twinkled, illuminating the path leading up to the entrance, where "Music Hall" was spelled out in bright, blazing bulbs. A warm, inviting glow lit up the pink-and-white canvas top and sides of the tent, and rousing music could be heard coming from within.

As Jack had warned, there were birds—and many other kinds of animals—dressed in fancy clothes, lined up to buy tickets. More lights decorated the smaller booths that bordered the path.

The group climbed down from the carriage and approached the line. In front of the entrance, a tall thin wolf wearing a fur-trimmed coat stood next to a plump badger in a green coat and a skinny weasel wearing a yellow bow tie. The badger had a pair of wire-rimmed glasses perched on his nose, and the buttons on his vest strained against his large round body.

The wolf swung a pocket watch from one clawed

finger. "Hurry, hurry! Only a few seats left!" he called out to the crowd. "Get your tickets while you can! One night only, one night—" He stopped, spotting Mary Poppins. "Mary Poppins! What an honor it is to have you join us this evening."

"Thank you," Mary Poppins replied with a polite nod.

"And who is this I see?" the wolf asked, peering around her toward the children. "Why, it's John, Annabel, and Georgie Banks!"

"You know us?" John asked, surprised.

"Of course!" the wolf said with a laugh. "*Everyone* knows the Banks children."

The badger nodded. "We've been watching you in the nursery for years," he said.

"It's so good to finally meet you," the weasel told the children sincerely.

"Get yourself some peanuts and candy floss and go right on in," the wolf told the children, handing them several tickets for treats.

Georgie looked up at Mary Poppins. "May we, Mary Poppins?" he asked.

Mary Poppins nodded. "Just be careful to keep away from the edge of the bowl."

The children glanced up at the starry sky above them. It looked like just a regular sky. They shrugged to each other and then dashed over to the candy floss booth, where they traded their tickets for paper cones covered in colorful spun sugar.

The children rejoined Mary Poppins and Jack, and the group entered the tent. Inside, it seemed larger than it had appeared from the outside, and it was quite grand, with red velvet curtains lining the walls. Several groups of box seats looked down on the dozens of rows spanning the floor. Up on the stage, a dancing troupe of flamingos performed an opening number while an orangutan in a tuxedo conducted the animal orchestra in the pit below.

Jack led Mary Poppins and the children to the front row. John entered first but went in one seat too far and nearly squashed a pair of hedgehogs. John was mortified, but the gentleman hedgehog gave him a forgiving smile, and the lady hedgehog gestured to the empty seat next to them. John squinted to make sure there was nothing smaller there—a parakeet, perhaps, or a tiny mouse— but it seemed safe and he sat down. He was relieved when he didn't hear anything—or anyone—cry out.

Annabel and Georgie sat down next to John, and Jack and Mary Poppins sat on the end. The flamingo showgirls finished up their number, and the audience applauded, paws and wings slapping together enthusiastically.

The lights dimmed and a drumroll sounded from the orchestra. A spotlight hit the stage—revealing Jack, who was now wearing a pink-and-purple suit. But instead of a top hat, he wore a bowler. Georgie glanced next to him, where Jack had just been sitting, and sure enough the seat was empty. Georgie placed Gillie down on the empty seat, next to Mary Poppins, and turned back to the stage, excited.

"Bucks and mares, cubs and does, welcome to our show of shows!" Jack announced. "It is my great honor to introduce this evening's special guest. The one . . . the only . . . *Mary Poppins!*"

Jack darted to the edge of the stage and held out his hand toward Mary Poppins. The spotlight shifted over to her, and the crowd cheered.

Mary Poppins smiled, flattered. She shrugged, as if it was pointless to argue, and allowed Jack to guide her up to the stage.

"Sing for us, Mary Poppins!" someone called out. Others repeated the request.

"You know the song they want," Jack whispered to her.

Mary Poppins shook her head. "I haven't sung that in years."

Behind her, four penguins in tuxedos peeked out between the curtains at the back of the stage. "Please, Mary Poppins?" begged one of the penguins.

"*Please*," echoed the others.

"No, no, I couldn't possibly," she insisted—but then, in the next moment, she leaned toward the conductor. "D-flat major," she told the orangutan. He nodded and raised his baton. The animal musicians picked up their instruments, ready to begin.

Jack stepped aside, leaving Mary Poppins alone in the spotlight. The curtains behind her parted partway, revealing a giant book, propped up and open, with the spine facing forward. A bowler hat hung from one corner, with a hooked cane next to it.

The penguins pushed the book forward, and Mary Poppins stepped behind it, disappearing from view. She tossed her dress over the top of the book and reached up to take down the bowler hat and the cane.

A few seconds passed, and then the giant book slid off into the wings, revealing Mary Poppins, now dressed in striped stockings, a frilly skirt, and a satin jacket, all in pinks and purples to match Jack's outfit.

The curtains parted completely, exposing several towering stacks of giant books. The penguins took down one of the books and propped it up so that it faced forward. Mary Poppins gestured to the book's cover, which had an illustration of a beautiful forest. She nodded to the penguins, who carefully laid the book down flat. They picked up the cover, and as they opened the book, a detailed Victorian street popped up from its pages.

Georgie and the twins, along with the rest of the audience, gasped in surprise. The cover had suggested the story inside would be medieval and magical—a dark, serious tale of knights and dragons or witches and spells. Instead, the setting was bright and realistic.

Jack nodded to the conductor, and as he helped Mary Poppins onto the stage's pop-up street, the orchestra launched into a lively dance hall tune. Jack jumped up beside Mary Poppins and they danced and sang to the music, twirling around the stiff paper figures.

"Let's show them another!" Jack said at the end of the song. The penguins helped Jack open another book, and a glittering royal palace rose from the pages. The orchestra's tune changed to a waltz. Jack took Mary Poppins in his arms and they danced gracefully around the pages, ducking in and out of the frozen royalty, who seemed to be staring curiously at the fancifully dressed interlopers.

Annabel thought about the books she'd read. It was true that the cover did sometimes suggest one type of story only to have the pages inside reveal a very different one.

This happened in life, too. A situation might not be quite what it first appeared to be. A person might turn out to be the opposite of what you'd thought when you first met them. Even bathtubs and porcelain bowls were not always what they appeared and could prove to be different—much, much different—from what they initially seemed.

Annabel and her brothers watched as the performance continued. The penguins waddled around the stage, opening the other books, and from all of them, entire worlds appeared, so very different from their covers. Mary Poppins and Jack dashed from book to book, changing their musical style to match the setting inside as the orchestra struggled to keep up. Once Mary Poppins and Jack had danced through every book, the penguins pushed the stacks into the wings, and they all vanished behind the curtain at the side of the stage.

The stage was now empty and the tent was silent— but only for a moment. Another book magically floated forward from the back of the stage and opened on its own. A grand staircase popped out from inside, rising to the rafters.

The music started again. At the top of the staircase appeared a chorus line of animals, arms hooked together, with Mary Poppins in the middle. As the conductor led the orchestra in a rousing number, the dancers made their way down the steps, kicking out their legs in unison.

Jack ran onto the stage and Mary Poppins broke from the chorus line. As Jack raced up the stairs, Mary Poppins marched down, joining him. The two linked arms and led the other dancers down the steps until they all reached the stage. They performed a final kick line as the music built to a crescendo, then ended, at last, with a thrilling cymbal crash.

The audience burst out of their seats, giving the dancers a standing ovation. Annabel and John stood up and clapped, exchanging grins, both thinking the same thing: even Mary Poppins herself had turned out to be nothing like she seemed "on the cover."

Georgie reached down to grab Gillie and lift him up to join in the applause—only to discover the giraffe was gone. He searched the floor, but there was no sign of the stuffed animal. Georgie climbed atop his seat and gazed around the tent, spotting shadows moving along one of the canvas walls. There was a silhouette of a wolf, swinging his pocket watch, and the outline of a weasel, carrying a large object. A badger-shaped shadow followed, with a smaller item in his hands—an item that was the exact same shape and size as Georgie's toy giraffe.

CHAPTER
14

"Gillie!" Georgie cried. He then hopped down from his seat and raced up the aisle.

Mary Poppins and Jack were still taking their bows. As the twins continued to clap, Annabel caught sight of the empty seat next to her. "Where's Georgie?" she asked John. She and John looked around and saw Georgie just as he was slipping through a tent flap at the side of the Music Hall.

Annabel grabbed John's hand. "Come on!" she shouted. They made their way down the row and hurried after their brother.

Outside the tent, Georgie had spotted the wolf, along with the badger and the weasel. The animals were loading up the back of a wagon with various items—which Georgie instantly recognized. They were all things from the Bankses' nursery! Toys, clothes—even the chairs and beds.

Georgie ran over to them. "What are you doing?" he demanded.

The wolf peered down at Georgie. "Well, well. If it isn't the boy who cracked the bowl." The wolf smiled coldly. "We've waited a long time for you Banks children to come and visit us—so *we* could pay a visit to your nursery."

"Those are *our* things!" Georgie said, pointing to the items in the wagon.

"Not anymore, they aren't," the wolf replied. He spun the crank at the front of the wagon, starting up the steam engine that powered the vehicle.

Georgie noticed Gillie inside the wagon and reached out to grab him. The badger tried to snatch the giraffe out of Georgie's hands, but Georgie wouldn't let go. "He's mine!" Georgie cried. "My mother made him for me!" The badger finally gave up trying to retrieve the giraffe, and he and the weasel picked up Georgie and tossed him into the wagon.

John and Annabel had exited the tent and spotted Georgie. "Leave our brother alone!" Annabel yelled.

"Time to go, boys!" the wolf shouted from the driver's seat. As the twins raced toward the wagon, the badger and the weasel leapt into the front with the wolf, and the wagon took off. Annabel and John chased after it but fell quickly behind as the wagon's engine exhaust engulfed them in a smoky cloud.

Georgie gripped the wooden slats of the wagon. "Let me go!" he screamed. "I want to go home!"

"What home?" the wolf yelled back. "You've lost your home!"

The wagon was going too fast for Annabel and John to keep up, and the vehicle soon vanished into the darkness ahead. The lights of the Music Hall were far behind them now, and the trees hid the moon and the stars. As the twins leaned over to catch their breath, they heard a clip-clop on the cobblestones behind them. A carriage appeared, and in the driver's seat sat a tall Irish setter in a coachman's uniform.

"Shamus!" Annabel cried.

The carriage stopped next to the twins. John and Annabel quickly climbed in, and Clyde took off. "Let's go get your brother back!" the horse shouted as he galloped down the path.

The carriage raced over the cobblestones, following the road as it curved up and down the sides of the porcelain bowl. Soon the wagon was again in sight.

"We're gaining on them!" yelled Shamus.

In the front of the wagon, the wolf heard Shamus's call and the sound of Clyde's hooves on the cobblestones. The wolf ordered the badger to shovel more coal into the steam engine. In the back of the wagon, Georgie held tight to Gillie as the two of them were thrown to the side of the speeding wagon, which was starting to tip.

The carriage caught up to the wagon and then moved alongside it. John and Annabel held the sides of the carriage as they carefully stood up.

"Ready?" John said. Annabel nodded. "Now!" he cried. They jumped out of the carriage, landing on the side of the wagon.

"Well done, children!" Shamus called to them as the carriage pulled away. "Good luck!"

Annabel peered in through the wagon's slats. "Are

you all right?" she asked Georgie. He nodded, clutching Gillie close.

The wolf spotted the twins. "Get rid of them!" he yelled to the weasel.

"But, sir—" the weasel protested.

"You heard me!" the wolf said.

The weasel and the badger climbed out of the cab and nervously crawled along the side toward the children. Annabel reached through the slats and grabbed her old cricket bat. When the badger and the weasel were close enough, she swung the bat at them but lost her grip, and it flew off. There was a loud *PING!* as the bat hit the side of the bowl, chipping off a piece of the porcelain. The chip hit the badger, throwing him off-balance. He tumbled into the weasel, knocking both of them off of the careening wagon.

"Well done!" John said. Annabel smiled. "I'll take care of the wolf," he continued. "You stay with Georgie."

Annabel nodded and climbed over the side of the wagon, then dropped inside. She gave Georgie a hug, and they both watched, tense, as John crawled toward the front of the wagon.

The wolf grabbed the shovel used for the coal and

swung it at John, but John ducked and the wolf missed, hitting the bowl and causing a deep crack to form along the side of it.

John arrived at an opening between the back of the wagon and the cab. He reached into the gap and unlatched the hook that attached the cab to the wagon. The cab and wagon separated, with the cab racing ahead toward a bridge, and the wagon rolling back down the hill. The cab crashed through the side of the bridge, throwing the wolf out. He landed in the muck below as the cab crashed into the water next to him.

John climbed over the slats into the back of the wagon and joined Annabel and Georgie. The wagon had gained speed as it rolled backward, and it swerved right and left like a runaway roller coaster. Its wheels hit the crack the wolf had made, causing the wagon to fly up the side of the bowl.

"Oh, no!" Annabel cried. She pointed ahead to a sign warning them they were about to reach the edge of the bowl. They all screamed as the wagon careened off the bowl's lip, soaring out into space, twisting and turning as it began to fall. . . .

Georgie gasped and sat up. He wasn't falling and he

wasn't in the wagon. He was in his bed, once again in his pajamas.

"It's quite all right," Mary Poppins said softly. She was sitting next to him and she brushed his hair away from his forehead. "You've been having a *nice* sort of nightmare, I'd say."

Georgie threw his arms around her and hugged her. "You were right," he told her. "A cover is *not* a book. We thought they were nice, but they were mean."

"Whatever are you talking about?" Mary Poppins said.

"They tried to take Gillie!" Georgie told her.

"Gillie is right here, sleeping." Mary Poppins patted the head of the toy giraffe, which was nestled against Georgie's pillow. "And so should you be." She lifted up the covers, and Georgie scooted under them.

"But it was real," Georgie insisted as Mary Poppins tucked him in. "They stole all our things, and the wolf said we were never going to see our home again."

Mary Poppins sniffed dismissively. "That's absurd," she said.

John, who had been listening to the conversation, sat up in his bed. "I had a nightmare like that, too," he said.

"So did I," Annabel said from her bed. "It seemed awfully real."

Georgie hugged Gillie, still thinking about the wolf. "I don't want to lose our home," he said.

John crossed to Georgie and sat down next to him. "That's why we wanted Mother's bowl," John told his brother. "We were going to sell it to save the house."

Georgie didn't want to lose the house, but he didn't want to lose anything that had belonged to his mother, either. "I miss Mother," he said softly.

Annabel hurried over, and the three children embraced each other, each trying to reassure the other two, despite their own doubts.

Mary Poppins looked down at the children a moment. "Listen to the three of you," she said, the gentle tone in her voice belying the sternness in her words. "You're all worrying far too much. After all, you can't lose what you never lost."

The children glanced up at Mary Poppins, puzzled.

"I don't understand," Georgie said.

"Your memories—all the people, places, and things in your life—remain forever," Mary Poppins explained. "Whoever you're missing, they still live inside you."

Mary Poppins parted the curtains in the front window. High up in the sky, a single bright star shone its light through the glass, onto the children. "She might even be smiling down at you from a star, watching you as you grow up, and looking out for you."

Annabel gazed up at the star. Could her mother really be up there? Was she really watching over them? It was a fanciful notion—but there was something in the warm light from the star that made Annabel sense the star was purposely shining directly down on them—and shining *for* them.

Mary Poppins gestured for the twins to return to their beds. "Every time you go to sleep," she told them as she tucked them in, "there's a chance you'll dream of one of the 'somethings' you thought you'd lost. And, in that way, it will be found again."

Mary Poppins tucked Georgie in one last time. "Now get some sleep," she told the children. "Tomorrow morning, bright and early, we'll take that bowl to my cousin and have it mended."

Mary Poppins closed the curtains but left a gap wide enough to let in the light from the star she had pointed toward.

Once Mary Poppins had left the nursery, Annabel turned on her side. The light from the star had landed on the bowl, which was once again on the mantel. Annabel leapt out of bed and hurried over to it.

"John! Come look!" she whispered as she carefully took down the bowl. John quietly got out of bed and tiptoed to Annabel's side. Annabel pointed to the illustration on the bowl. "Mary Poppins's scarf," she said.

John took the bowl and held it up to the light. There, in the painting of the carriage, was the very scarf, tied around the wheel.

"It wasn't a dream," Annabel said.

John glanced toward the door to Mary Poppins's room. "Shall we tell her?" he asked.

Annabel shook her head. "I expect she already knows."

CHAPTER
15

Early the next morning, after wheeling the admiral out to the roof-deck, Mr. Binnacle blew his whistle: *TWEET!* "Admiral above deck!" he announced.

Below, Jack glanced up from the top of his ladder, which was propped against the streetlamp at number 17. He could see Admiral Boom, sitting at attention in his wheelchair. The admiral's eyes were on the pocket watch he held in one hand, and his other hand grasped the rope to the cannon as he got ready to fire.

"*BONG! BONG! BONG!...*" Big Ben rang in the distance, beginning its eight o'clock toll.

"Blast it!" cried Admiral Boom, enraged. "Too soon! Why can't those pea-brained Big Ben buffoons get it right?" The admiral spotted Jane coming down the lane, a large stack of rally flyers in her arms, and his bad mood vanished. Admiral Boom was always pleased to see any member of the Banks family. They'd always been respectful neighbors and had never once complained about his cannon. They knew he was carrying out important work. "Ahoy, fair lady!" he called down.

"Good morning!" Jane shouted up to him. She didn't see Jack sliding down the lamp pole—and Jack didn't notice Jane taking a step forward. The lamplighter collided with the activist, and Jane's flyers went flying.

"I am so sorry, miss!" Jack said.

"It's all right," Jane assured him. She couldn't help noticing that he was quite handsome.

"You're Miss Banks, aren't you?" Jack said as he helped Jane gather up the flyers. "I don't know if you remember me, but I used to wave to you when I'd see you and your brother up there in that window." He nodded up toward the Bankses' nursery.

"I *do* remember." Jack had been handsome then, too. "Please. Call me Jane." She blushed and focused on arranging her flyers—and therefore she didn't notice Jack blushing as well.

Inside the front entry hall of number 17, Ellen spied on Jack and Jane through a crack in the front door.

"Polishing the keyhole?" Mary Poppins asked as she came down the stairs behind Ellen.

Ellen gestured toward the street. "Miss Jane's chattin' with that 'andsome lamplighter. Looks as though he's lit 'er up as well. Not that anything'll ever come of it. She says that ship has sailed."

Mary Poppins reached Ellen and closed the door. "And *I* say there are always other ships," she told the housekeeper.

A moment later, Michael raced down the stairs, his briefcase in hand. "My alarm clock didn't ring!" he said in a panic. "I'm going to be late!"

"You're not late yet," Mary Poppins said calmly. "Let me help you." She took Michael's briefcase and gave it to Ellen and then handed Michael his coat. While Michael hurriedly put it on, Mary Poppins retrieved his hat and umbrella.

"Off you go!" Mary Poppins said, handing Michael the hat and umbrella and then ushering him out the door. "John! Annabel! Georgie!" she called up the stairs. "Spit-spot!"

Outside, Michael raced past Jack and Jane. "I have to run, forgive me!" He dashed down the street, dodging passersby. Jane shook her head with a laugh as her brother disappeared around the corner.

Soon after, Mary Poppins, followed by the three children, emerged from the house, holding a canvas bag. "Good morning, Jane," she said. "The children and I are heading into town. Would you like to come with us?"

Jane shook her head. "I can't, I'm afraid." She held up her flyers. "We have a rally today."

Mary Poppins nodded toward Jack. "You should give Jack one of those flyers."

Jane pulled one from the stack and offered it to Jack. "The rally is this afternoon, if you can come," she said.

"'SPRUCE,' eh?" Jack said, reading the flyer. "Good for you, Jane Banks. All of us lamplighters know what a fine job you're doing for the workers. Fighting the good fight."

Jane smiled, flattered. "We do our best," she said.

Inside the Bankses' house, Ellen had returned to the

kitchen—only to realize she still had Michael's briefcase in her arms. She raced back through the hall and out the door. "Mr. Banks forgot his briefcase," she told Mary Poppins. She shook her head. "He'd leave his head on the breakfast table if it weren't screwed on."

"Give it to me," Mary Poppins replied, taking the briefcase from Ellen. "The children and I are heading that way on an errand and we can stop by the bank afterwards."

"I'll give you a lift on my bicycle," Jack offered. "My rounds are done."

"Wonderful!" Mary Poppins said.

"But there are five of us," Annabel pointed out. "We can't all fit."

"Oh, yes, we can," Jack said. He fastened his ladder on the back of his bicycle, perpendicular to the rear fender, so that the ladder reached out in either direction like the wings of an airplane. "All aboard!" he said with a wave.

John did some calculations in his head. "The weight on those wheels alone . . ." He shook his head, certain Jack's idea was impossible. He turned to Mary Poppins. "Mary Poppins, how much do you weigh?"

Mary Poppins stared at John in shock and disapproval. It was very rude to ask a woman her weight. She opened her mouth to scold him, but Jack quickly intervened.

"Never you mind about that," Jack told John. "It's a question of balance." Jack turned to Georgie. "You'll be in front." Mary Poppins placed the briefcase in the large front basket of the bike as a pillow, and Jack lifted Georgie and settled him in on top of it, cross-legged.

Mary Poppins then held the bike steady as Jack helped Annabel onto one side of the ladder and boosted John up next to her.

Jane watched Jack transform his bike into a bus. "Are you quite sure this is safe?" she asked Mary Poppins.

"Not in the slightest," Mary Poppins replied as Jack switched places with her. He held the handlebars as she hopped onto the other side of the ladder while placing the canvas bag on her lap. "Sit up straight," she told the twins. "You're not flour bags." The twins straightened up their posture.

Jane decided not to argue. Mary Poppins had been trustworthy when she and Michael were young. There was no reason not to trust her now.

Jack climbed onto the bike and tipped his cap to Jane. "You ever need a ladder raised or lamp lit, Miss Jane, consider it done."

Jane smiled. "Thank you, Jack."

Up on the roof-deck, Admiral Boom turned to his first mate. "Primed and ready, Mr. Binnacle?" Admiral Boom asked.

"Ready as charged, sir!"

The admiral began his countdown: "Three . . . two . . . one . . ."

Down on the street, Jack glanced over his shoulder. "Ready, everyone?"

"Ready!" said Mary Poppins.

"Ready!" the children called out together.

Jack stood up on the pedals. "Steady . . ."

BOOM! the cannon thundered.

"Go!" Jack yelled. He pushed down on the pedals, struggling for a moment to keep the bicycle upright. But he soon found the perfect balance, and the bike sailed down Cherry Tree Lane as Jane and Ellen waved goodbye.

CHAPTER 16

Georgie grinned, the wind blowing across his face, as Jack pedaled his passengers through the London streets. They'd only just had breakfast and they were already off on another adventure!

"Pull over ahead," Mary Poppins called up to Jack. Jack slowed the bike, stopping at the entrance to a narrow alley, and Mary Poppins and the twins hopped off the ladder.

"Never noticed this alley before," Jack said as he lifted Georgie from the basket. Georgie peered down the narrow lane, intrigued by the colorful shops on both sides.

"Clearly you've never had a porcelain bowl that wanted mending," Mary Poppins told Jack. She held up the canvas bag in her hand and then used it to shoo the children toward the alley. "Off we go, jiggety-jog."

Jack tagged along as they strolled past the shop windows, where all manner of interesting and unusual items were displayed. There was a shop just for inkwells, and one for buttons. There was another that sold maps, and one that seemed to contain nothing but dictionaries, large and small, old and new, in every language imaginable.

"Here we are!" Mary Poppins said when they'd reached a tiny doorway at the very end of the alley. The door was so low the top of the frame barely reached the top of Georgie's head.

Annabel leaned down to read the sign above the door. "'Topotrepolovsky's Restorations and Fix-It Shop. All Repairs Large and Small.'"

"Looks as though it's just a *small* fix-it shop today," Jack said with a grin.

Mary Poppins patted the canvas bag. "That's exactly what we want," she said. "The bowl only needs a small fix, after all." She rapped on the door with the parrot head of her umbrella.

"So now my head is a door knocker?" the parrot squawked. "I suppose my beak might be useful for opening cans, and—"

"Fuss, fuss, fuss," Mary Poppins said tersely. "Don't be so dramatic." She rapped on the door again, but there was no answer. She pushed the tip of the umbrella into the letter box slot. "Cousin Topsy?" she called through the slot.

"No, Mary Poppins! Stop!" yelled someone from inside the shop. "For the love of all that is holy, do not come in!" It was a woman's voice, high-pitched and operatic, with an unusual European accent.

"Don't be rude!" Mary Poppins replied through the slot.

"Stay away, please," the voice insisted. "It is Second Wednesday!"

Mary Poppins straightened up. "Oh, dear, I'd forgotten." She thought a moment and then shrugged. "Still, today or never—that's my motto." She forced the sharp tip of her umbrella into the keyhole and whacked the parrot on the top of the head.

"Ouch!" protested the parrot.

Mary Poppins ignored the parrot and twisted the

umbrella, opening the lock. She pushed open the door. "Follow me," she told the others.

Jack and the children ducked through the doorway after Mary Poppins. As they stepped into the shop's foyer, the door magically grew to normal size. But a bigger surprise awaited them.

The space was cluttered with hundreds of broken objects piled up to the rafters—or rather piled *down*. For the entire shop was upside down! A spiral staircase stood in the middle of the room, leading up—or rather *down*—to a woman in exotic clothing, who was standing upside down. Or was she right side up and it was the visitors who were upside down?

It was hard to know what was up or down, which was right or wrong. Gravity didn't seem to work in the shop—or rather it worked too well. Although the shop had flipped, the objects and furniture hadn't fallen down, nor had the woman. Yet Mary Poppins and the others didn't fall up, either.

"So in you come," the woman said with a wounded tone. "You do not listen to Topsy."

"You have guests, Cousin," Mary Poppins said sternly. "You might at least greet them at the door."

"And how might I do this, please," asked Topsy, "when I am down here on the ceiling—or rather up on the floor, which is now the ceiling, while you are on the ceiling, which is now the floor?"

Mary Poppins sighed. "Very well, we'll come to you." She gestured to the children. "Be careful on the way . . . up."

Mary Poppins made her way up—or down—carefully stepping around the broken objects littering the steps. Jack and the children followed.

"Why be careful?" cried Topsy, noticing how her guests were approaching, and then throwing a hand to her forehead. "Climb on my shelves! Step on the toys! Kick the little china dolls in their faces!"

Mary Poppins rolled her eyes. "John, Annabel, Georgie, Jack," she said with a note of exasperation. "This is my cousin."

"*Second* cousin," Topsy corrected. "*Many* times removed."

"Tatiana Antanasia Cositori Topotrepolovsky," Mary Poppins continued, ignoring Topsy's comment.

Topsy curtsied. "You may call me Topsy," she said.

As they got closer, the children saw that Topsy's

outfit seemed to have been fashioned out of items from her shop. Her sweater was a patchwork of velvet and ribbon scraps. Her earrings were the tassels from curtain pulls, and her necklace was made of pencil stubs that were strung together. Topsy's shoulder-length red hair was held back by a brocade scarf, kept in place by two long skinny paintbrushes.

"That's an unusual accent you've got there," Jack said. "Where are you from?"

Topsy gazed up at the ceiling—or rather the floor. "Well . . ."

"We have no idea," Mary Poppins said, answering Jack. Topsy's background was a bit of a mystery and one that it had always seemed wiser not to look into too carefully. To change the subject, Mary Poppins removed the bowl from the canvas bag and held it out to her cousin.

"No, no!" Topsy protested, throwing up her hands and backing away from the bowl. "It is, as I have told you, the second Wednesday of the month, when everything goes kerflooey!"

"What exactly does that mean?" Annabel asked.

Topsy leaned down to Annabel. "Sweet girl, you tell

Mary Poppins, who doesn't listen, that any other day, Tatiana Antanasia Cositori Topotrepolovsky can fix *anything*." She straightened up and waved to the objects around her. "If you brought me a ripped sweater on a Thursday, I could sew it up quickly," she explained. "If you brought me a broken lamp on a Friday, I could glue it together."

Topsy began to climb, gesturing as she made her way down to the ceiling. "On a Saturday, I could return a heel to a shoe. I could mend a marionette on a Sunday, or repair a ripped book on a Monday. On a Tuesday, I could make a broken toy return to life. But on a Wednesday . . ." Topsy clasped her hands together and shook her head, causing her gold tassel earrings to swing like little grass skirts. "Every *second* Wednesday, that is, from nine to noon, the world turns turtle—and my life turns upside down!"

Topsy twirled around, gesturing to the ceiling below her and the floor above. "Everything is opposite, you see. Below is above, under is over, behind is before." She threw her arms up toward the floor. "Up is down!" she cried. She bowed toward the ceiling. "And down is up."

She raced back up—or rather down—until she reached the children. "It is simply the way of every second Wednesday." Topsy paused, as if waiting for her guests to ask her more about the difficulties of her topsy-turvy life.

Jack, guessing Topsy's desire, spotted a pile of instruments nearby and picked up a drum. "Could you fix a drum?" he asked, banging lightly on its rim.

Topsy shook her head sadly.

John joined the game, grabbing a clarinet. "How about the clarinet?" he asked.

Topsy threw her hands over her face in despair. Jack and John exchanged grins.

Annabel smiled and lifted up a large string bass. "I guess you can't fix this, either," she said, plucking a warped string.

Topsy peered between her fingers. "Well, *perhaps* . . . if you helped me."

Jack and the children glanced at Mary Poppins. "Very well," Mary Poppins said with a nod. She set down the bowl and picked up a quill pen to use as a conductor's baton. Jack handed Georgie a xylophone, and under Mary Poppins's direction, the makeshift orchestra began to play.

Topsy danced around the group, not seeming to notice their off-key notes or stilted rhythm. As they continued to bang and blow and pluck, their playing magically improved and the instruments repaired themselves.

When the tune reached its final notes, Topsy suddenly floated up and flipped around. "I'm right side up!" she declared. "How is this possible?"

"Sometimes you need to consider things from another point of view," Mary Poppins told her. "And you know as well as I that everything is possible. Even the impossible."

"But now I am topsy-turvy," Topsy said.

"I wouldn't mind seeing things from another angle," Jack said, watching Topsy turn cartwheels in the air.

"May we?" Annabel asked Mary Poppins. If anyone could find a way for them to fly and float from ceiling to floor and back, it would be Mary Poppins.

"Very well. Flippity-flop," Mary Poppins said as she tossed her umbrella into the air. The umbrella popped open and spun around, and the children felt themselves lift off. Jack and Mary Poppins followed, and the whole group flipped and twirled, heads over heels, before finally landing on their feet next to Topsy on the ceiling near the door.

"I must say, Wednesdays are now my favorite day!" Topsy declared. "Thank you, Cousin Mary!"

Mary Poppins nodded modestly.

"Give your bowl to Topsy," Topsy said. "No more am I afraid with this new point of view."

Mary Poppins had grabbed the bowl when the spinning started, and she now handed it to Topsy.

"Do you have any idea how much our bowl might be worth?" John asked.

Topsy studied the bowl, peering at it from every angle. "Not much at all, I'm afraid," she said finally. "But that doesn't make it any less beautiful."

"But our mother said it was priceless," Annabel protested.

"I'm sure it was. To her," Topsy said kindly. She could see the disappointment in the children's eyes. "Cousin Mary is right, for once," Topsy told them. "It is all in the way you look at things."

"Thank you, Cousin," Mary Poppins said. "Come along, children." She ushered the children toward the door.

"Nice meeting you, Topsy Turvy," Jack said.

"'Topsy Turvy'!" echoed Topsy. "I like it! It's catchy."

"Now what do we do?" Annabel whispered to John as the group returned to the alley. If their bowl wasn't worth anything, they wouldn't be able to make any money from it, even if Topsy could repair it.

John shrugged, defeated. "I have no idea," he said.

"Well, we need to think of something fast," Annabel told him. "We only have two more days."

As if to remind the twins of how quickly time was passing, Big Ben began to toll in the distance, ringing out the noon hour. A moment later, a loud crash came from inside Topsy's shop. "Marvelous," Mary Poppins said. "It sounds as though things are starting to turn around for my cousin."

John and Annabel exchanged curious glances. Had the items in the shop fallen right side up or upside down? They both shrugged. There was no way to know.

"Can we go back and visit Cousin Topsy again soon?" Georgie asked as they reached the end of the alley.

Jack glanced over his shoulder. "Looks as though

we might have to wait until the next Second Wednesday," he said. Georgie looked back as well, and his jaw dropped open in shock.

There was nothing but a large gray brick wall behind them. The alleyway had completely disappeared.

CHAPTER

17

The next stop was the bank. Mary Poppins navigated, telling Jack where to turn the bicycle and which direction to go. John consulted his pocket watch, concerned. They weren't taking the most efficient route.

"There's Aunt Jane!" Georgie shouted.

John looked up from his watch. Indeed, just ahead of them was their aunt Jane, walking briskly down the cobblestoned street, carrying an armload of rally posters and banners.

"Aunt Jane!" Annabel called out to her.

Jane turned around, smiling, as the group approached. "Hello, everyone!" she said.

"Off to the rally, are you, Jane?" Mary Poppins asked. Jane nodded.

Jack slowly braked and brought the bicycle to a stop next to Jane. "I say, I could come back and give you a hand with all that once I drop the others at the bank," he offered.

"Oh, no, please don't worry," Jane said. "I'm perfectly fine."

"Nonsense," Mary Poppins said. "The bank is just around the corner, and the children and I have plenty of legs to get us there." She hopped off the bike and held it steady as Annabel and John jumped down.

Jack lifted Georgie out of the basket and handed him Michael's briefcase. Jack then tied Jane's banners and posters to the ladder and set the flyers in the basket.

"You should ride in the basket," Georgie told Jane. He knew his aunt liked adventure as much as he did.

"I think she'll be better here," Jack said, patting the bar in front of the seat. "Steady the bicycle for me, would you, children?"

Annabel and John each grabbed a handlebar as Jack

helped settle Jane onto the bar sidesaddle and then climbed onto the seat behind her. "All right, you can let go," Jack told the twins. "Ready?" he asked Jane.

"As ready as I'll ever be," Jane said, holding tight to the handlebars.

Mary Poppins smiled and the children waved as the pair sailed off down the street. They heard Jane laughing with delight as the bicycle picked up speed.

Mary Poppins took the briefcase from Georgie and led the children around the corner to the bank. The street in front of the building was busy with people coming and going, paying little attention to the beautiful day—or to the nanny and three children making their way up the front steps to the grand doorway of Fidelity Fiduciary.

Inside the bank, the lobby was even more crowded and bustling than the street outside. People instinctively made way for Mary Poppins, however, as she marched straight across the marble lobby to the information desk. The children hurriedly followed her in a straight line, like ducklings following their mother.

They reached the desk to find the clerk busy dealing with a mail delivery. Mary Poppins waved the children to a nearby bench. "Go sit over there until I've taken care of this, and then we'll be on our way."

John helped Georgie onto the bench next to Annabel and then took a seat on the other side of her. "There must be someone at this bank who could help us save our house," John whispered to his sister.

"I'm sure Father already asked," Annabel said.

"*We* haven't." John recalled their experience at Topsy's. "Maybe we can get them to see things from a new point of view."

Annabel noticed Georgie waving to someone entering the bank. She glanced over to see Mr. Gooding and Mr. Frye. Mr. Frye smiled at Georgie and waved back. Annabel quickly pulled Georgie's hand down.

"What did you do that for?" Georgie asked Annabel. "You hurt his feelings."

Annabel saw Mr. Frye's smile vanish and his face cloud with guilt. He hunched over, following Mr. Gooding up the staircase at the far end of the lobby.

"You do know who those men are, don't you?" Annabel asked Georgie.

Georgie knew very well. "They're the lawyers," he said. "The one I waved to is the nice one."

CHAPTER 17

Annabel watched the lawyers disappear down a hallway on the upper level. Mr. Frye *did* seem to be the friendlier of the two men. She turned to John. "Maybe we could convince Mr. Frye to help us," she said.

John had been thinking the same thing. "Worth a try," he said, and stood up. "Today or never. That's my motto," he added, echoing Mary Poppins.

Annabel smiled. She and John each took one of Georgie's hands, and the three made their way across the crowded lobby to the staircase.

At the information desk, Mary Poppins smiled to herself as she watched the children hurry up the steps.

Once upstairs, the children followed Mr. Gooding and Mr. Frye down the hallway, to Mr. Wilkins's office. As the lawyers entered the outer office, the children crept up to the door. John peered in, but the lawyers had disappeared into the far office and closed the door behind them. He saw "Office of the Bank President" written on the inner door's frosted glass.

Mr. Wilkins's secretary regarded the young boy at the door curiously. "Is there something I can do for you, young man?" she asked.

Before John could answer, Georgie spotted the jar

of toffees on Miss Farthing's desk. "May I have a sweet, please?" he asked.

"Why, of course, dear," Miss Farthing said. She lifted the top of the jar and smiled at John—and at Annabel, who had poked in her head as well. Miss Farthing had just purchased the candies that morning. She'd been unsure why exactly Mr. Wilkins had asked her to get them, but she now saw that they were a nice asset when the bank's youngest customers came calling.

The children all approached the desk, and each took a piece of candy. As they unwrapped the sweets, they could hear muffled voices coming from behind the closed inner door. A moment later, the intercom on Miss Farthing's desk buzzed.

"Did I not ask for tea, Miss Farthing?" barked a voice from the speaker.

Miss Farthing pressed a button on the box. "Yes, sir," she said into the intercom. "Right away, Mr. Wilkins." She stood up and slid the toffee jar closer to the children. "Why don't you help yourselves while I go get the tea?" she said. "I'll be right back."

Annabel and John exchanged looks, and once Miss Farthing was out of sight, they tiptoed to the closed door. The twins pressed their ears against the wood, while Georgie attempted to peer in through the crack along the side.

"How many repossessions so far this month?" the children heard a man inside ask. They recognized it as the voice from the intercom. This, John realized, must be Mr. Wilkins, the bank president.

"Nineteen, sir," they heard Mr. Gooding reply. "And we have nearly that many scheduled for next week alone."

"Who would've thought this slump would be so good for business, eh?" Mr. Wilkins asked in a pleased tone of voice.

"I wonder, Mr. Wilkins, if, perhaps, as Michael Banks is an employee, you might consider giving him a few more weeks to pay off his loan?" The children recognized this voice as Mr. Frye's, and it confirmed their suspicion that he was a nicer man than the other two.

"And lose our chance to get that house?" Mr. Wilkins snapped. "I don't like to lose, Mr. Frye."

"It's just that, well, his family has faced tremendous hardship this past year," Mr. Frye countered.

Georgie stepped back and saw Mr. Wilkins's shadow appear through the cloudy glass pane at the top of the door. The shadow swung a pocket watch, looking very much like the shadow of the wolf Georgie had seen on the Music Hall tent the previous night.

"You're not giving Banks one second longer to pay off that loan," Mr. Wilkins said firmly. "I'm running a business, not a charity. In two days, Banks will be out on that street and the house will be ours. Do I make myself clear?"

Hearing this, Georgie opened the door and raced inside.

"Georgie, no!" John shouted, running after him.

Georgie ignored his brother and stomped up to Mr. Wilkins. "You can't steal our house!" he said, glaring up at the bank president. "I'm telling my father!"

Mr. Wilkins stared at Georgie, confused. "What are you talking about?" The twins hurried to Georgie's side. "Who are *you?*" Mr. Wilkins demanded.

"These are the Banks children," Mr. Frye explained.

"Ah," Mr. Wilkins said, putting away his pocket watch and donning a friendly smile. He leaned down toward the children. "I think you may have misunderstood."

John sensed the danger behind Mr. Wilkins's false

kindness and tugged on Georgie's arm. "Let's go," he said urgently.

Mr. Wilkins reached out a hand to stop the children. "Run!" cried Annabel, taking Georgie's other arm.

The children dashed out the door and through the outer office, nearly colliding with Miss Farthing and her tea tray. "Stop them!" shouted Mr. Wilkins.

The children's footsteps thundered as they sprinted down the hall toward the staircase and then raced down the steps to the lobby. They saw Mary Poppins handing their father his briefcase and hurried over to them.

"Father, help!" Georgie cried. "The wolf is trying to steal our house!" He pointed toward Mr. Wilkins, who was marching across the lobby toward them, followed by Mr. Gooding and Mr. Frye.

"What on earth are you talking about?" Michael asked.

"I'm afraid your children burst into my office just now, Banks," Mr. Wilkins said. "I was seeing if anything could be done about extending your loan when they charged in, claiming I was trying to steal your house."

"He *is* trying to steal it," Annabel insisted. "We heard him."

Michael shook his head. "Mr. Wilkins is trying to help us," he told the children.

"Then why was he chasing us?" John asked.

Mr. Wilkins dug into his coat pocket and pulled out a handful of toffees. "I thought they might stop running about and making a scene if I offered them some sweets." The children glared up at him. "Apparently, I was wrong."

"I'm so sorry, Mr. Wilkins," Michael said.

Mr. Wilkins nodded kindly. "Let's just see it doesn't happen again." He turned to the children. "After all, you don't want your father losing his job on account of you, do you?" The twins looked away, refusing to answer, but Georgie continued to glare.

Mr. Wilkins ignored Georgie and placed a hand on Michael's shoulder. "I want you to have every chance to pay off that loan, Banks," he said. "I'll stay in my office on Friday evening until the last stroke of midnight. You have my word."

Michael nodded, grateful. "Thank you, sir."

Mr. Wilkins gestured to the two lawyers. "Gentlemen,"

he said. The three men headed up the stairs, back to their offices.

Annabel tugged on her father's sleeve. "But, Father, he really is—"

"Not another word!" Michael snapped. "I can't tell you how disappointed I am in the three of you, behaving like that." He turned to Mary Poppins. "And you, Mary Poppins. You know better than to lose track of them."

"You're absolutely right," Mary Poppins agreed. "I do know better."

"Take them straight back to the house this instant," Michael ordered. "We'll talk about this when I get home."

"Yes, sir." Mary Poppins ushered the children through the busy lobby to the doors.

Outside, a damp gray fog had settled over the city— and a similar feeling of gloom had descended over the children as well.

CHAPTER
18

The fog grew thicker and the gray of the sky deepened as Mary Poppins and the Banks children made their way home through the city. Normally, John would be checking his pocket watch, predicting the time they'd arrive, but he wasn't in the mood. "Now we've done it, haven't we?" he grumbled, shuffling his feet over the cobblestones. "I don't think I've ever seen Father that upset with us before."

"But we were telling the truth!" Georgie protested.

"That doesn't matter, Georgie," Annabel said. She felt as despondent as John. "We got Father in trouble. And he doesn't even know we broke Mother's bowl yet." She pictured their father's face when he did see the cracked bowl, but then quickly pushed the image away. It was too upsetting to think about.

John sighed. "Everything we tried to fix we've only made worse."

The children continued through the fog, each one deep in thought. Mary Poppins followed, watching them closely. When they reached the end of the street, the fog was so thick it was difficult to make out the buildings around them. Even the street signs disappeared into the murky gray that had seemingly descended from above.

Annabel looked left and right, confused. "Which way do we go?" she asked Mary Poppins.

"Why ask me?" Mary Poppins replied. "The three of you are leading the way, after all."

"Us?" Annabel said. "But we were—"

"Walking around in a fog," Mary Poppins said, finishing the sentence for her.

"No, we weren't," Annabel said. "I mean, yes, we *are* in a fog, but—"

"We were only talking," John said, coming to his sister's defense.

Mary Poppins nodded. "Exactly. Too focused on where you've been to pay attention to where you're going."

"Father told us to go straight home," John reminded her.

"He'll be furious if we're late," added Annabel.

Mary Poppins shrugged. "Not much to be done about that now."

Georgie glanced around, worried. "Are we lost, Mary Poppins?"

"That would depend on where you want to go," a familiar voice called out from the mist. A light appeared, and it grew brighter as the children walked toward it. When they got close enough, the light revealed itself as a streetlamp, and there, at the top of his ladder, was Jack, smiling down at them. In his hand was the thin pole with the flame at the top that he used to light the lamps.

"Jack!" cried Georgie in delight.

Jack tipped his cap. "At your service." He peered at

the children as he climbed down the ladder. "What's with all the glum faces?" he asked. "Lost sixpence and found a penny?"

"We've made a mess of everything," Annabel told him.

"Father's furious with us," John said.

"And we can't find our way home," Georgie added.

"Lost?" Jack shook his head, not believing it. "Are you lost, Mary Poppins?"

"Hopelessly," she replied.

"Well, I'm no expert," Jack told the group, "but whenever I lose my way, I just look for a little light to guide me." He waved his pole toward a nearby lamp that had not yet been lit. "If you're ever lost, just look up," he continued. "There's always a light shining, or about to shine, somewhere up ahead." Jack moved his ladder to the lamp, climbed up, opened the glass door, and touched the flaming tip of his pole to the wick inside. "You can even pretend you're a *leerie* and shine the light yourself." The wick caught the flame and flared up, filling the glass lamp with a warm, inviting light, which cast a magical glow into the fog around it.

"What's a leerie?" asked John.

"It's what we lamplighters call ourselves," Jack explained. "And I believe it's time to send out the call to arms." He fiddled with the flame, making it brighter and then dimmer and then brighter again, sending out a signal. "Leeries!" he shouted as he continued to lower and raise the flame. "Trip the lights and lead the way!"

Up and down the street, lights appeared in the fog. They began far apart but then closed in, becoming a swarm of twinkling stars. As the lights grew nearer, they emerged from the fog, revealing a band of lamplighters, a dozen or more, waving their long, thin torches.

Jack leapt down from his ladder and danced ahead, gesturing for the leeries to follow. As they made their way down the street, the leeries hopped up to light the dark streetlamps one by one, bringing them to life.

"Never be afraid of the dark," Jack called out to the children as they ran to catch up. "Never be afraid of the dark, foggy night. Just light a light."

"You don't mind the dark at all?" Annabel asked Jack.

Jack shook his head. "Us leeries are more accustomed to the dark than most," he explained. "We love the twilight, when the sun is setting and the moon is rising, and the sky's revolving through its magical hues, from pink to purple to that deep, deep blue of night. To us, it's a bright time, because we get to light the lights."

As the group continued down the foggy streets, more leeries joined the pack, with Jack in the lead like a lamp-lighting Pied Piper. Soon the whole boulevard was lit up, and the dense fog was pushed away.

The children followed Jack and the leeries around a corner, where they reached a dead end. "Now what do we do?" John asked.

"Exactly what Jack said to do," replied Mary Poppins, and she stepped onto the base of the ornate streetlamp next to her. "We follow the light." The children watched in surprise as the base sank through the pavement, disappearing underground with Mary Poppins. The lamp and the pole, now several yards long, remained above, at street level.

Georgie ran to the side of the hole, eager to see where Mary Poppins had gone. Annabel and John quickly caught up to him and grabbed his hands, worried he might fall in. The three cautiously peered into the darkness and spotted Mary Poppins several feet below, waving at them to follow. John turned to Annabel and shrugged. They'd already followed their nanny into a magical ocean, a music hall hidden inside a porcelain bowl, and an upside-down shop. Following her underground seemed almost tame in comparison.

John grabbed the pole and slid down. Annabel helped Georgie onto the pole, and he slid down after John. Annabel then followed.

The three children reached the bottom of the pole and saw an entrance to a large drainpipe ahead of them. The voices of the leeries could be heard deep inside the tunnel, echoing against the concrete walls.

Mary Poppins and the children followed the voices through the pipe, arriving at last in an empty park. The streetlamps lining the park's pathways were dark and cast long silhouettes onto the ground. Mary Poppins led the children to a fountain in the center of the park. The fountain was dry and filled with dirt and leaves, like a relic from another time.

Annabel peered into the shadows around them. Where were the leeries? As if in answer, the lamps along the pathways flickered on one by one, each revealing a leerie at its base, torch in hand. Soon the entire park was glowing with brilliant light.

Jack pedaled into view on his bicycle. The children

cheered as he kicked up his legs, performing a head-stand. He held on tight to the handlebars, which he used to steer past them.

The other leeries retrieved their bicycles from behind the lamps and joined Jack. They sped along the paths, leaping from one side of their bikes to the other, executing the kinds of tricks the children had seen circus acrobats perform with horses.

Georgie and the twins applauded. One of the leeries, a skinny young man with black curly hair, called out to them. "Join us in a bit of kick and prance!" he urged.

"What did he say?" John asked Jack, confused.

Jack hopped down from his bicycle. "Angus was sharing a bit of leerie-speak," he explained. "'Kick and prance' means 'dance.' You don't say the word you mean. Instead, you say something that rhymes." Georgie and the twins cocked their heads at him, still puzzled. "We'll show you how it works." Jack nodded to Angus.

"Give us your weep and wail," said Jack. He leaned over to the children. "That means 'tale.'"

"I was short a sheet," said Angus.

"He was in the street," translated Jack. "You see?" he said. "There's nothing to it."

"Can you speak leerie?" Annabel asked Mary Poppins.

Mary Poppins looked at Annabel in shock. "Can *I* speak leerie?"

"Of course she can," said Jack. "She's Mary Poppins!"

"Can we do it with you?" Georgie asked.

"Please?" Annabel and John begged in unison.

"Oh, very well," Mary Poppins said. Jack lifted Mary Poppins onto the lip of the fountain, and the other leeries gathered around.

"Go on, then," Jack said to the children. "Tell us your sorry tale."

"Give us your weep and wail," said Angus in leerie-speak.

Annabel nodded to John to start. "Um, well, we had this bowl . . ." John began.

"Rabbit in the hole," said Mary Poppins, translating.

"That fell and broke," Annabel continued.

"Bicycle spoke." Mary Poppins tiptoed along the fountain ledge, with the children and leeries following.

The leerie-speak rhyming game continued, with even Georgie chiming in. Mary Poppins walked faster, and the children hurried to keep up.

Mary Poppins stopped and waved her arms. Behind

her the fountain magically came to life, sending sparkling jets of water into the air.

The children laughed and clapped. Their dark mood had lifted at last.

"You've got it!" Jack said. "Now let's get you back down the drain!"

"To Cherry Tree Lane!" the children shouted in unison.

Jack grinned and tossed his leerie pole into the air.

CHAPTER

19

Annabel looked around, stunned. They were no longer in the park but instead were now at the far end of Cherry Tree Lane. It was still foggy, however, the mist so thick that there was no sign of the moon. The tops of the streetlamps were hazy glowing orbs, their outlines lost in the murky night.

Jack and the leeries were still with the group, and they used their torches to lead Mary Poppins and the children through the fog toward number 17.

"We're almost home," Georgie said.

"Brush and comb," John replied in leerie-speak, and all three children giggled. Their laughter was cut short, however, when the door to their house flew open and Michael stepped out, an angry frown on his face.

"Where on earth have you all been?" Michael demanded. He turned his glare toward Mary Poppins. "I told you to bring them straight home. I've been worried sick."

"We're sorry we're late, Father," Annabel said. "It wasn't Mary Poppins's fault."

"We got lost in the fog," John said.

"Jack and the leeries led us home down the frog and toad," added Georgie. He waved behind them, but all of the leeries except for Jack had mysteriously vanished into the fog. The wicks of their lamp-lighting poles blinked off, disappearing like fireflies into the night.

"He means 'road,'" Mary Poppins said, translating for Michael.

Michael frowned at her. "So you've been off filling the children's heads with nonsense." He shook his head, annoyed and frustrated. It had been a long, difficult day, and his temper was near the breaking point. He ordered the children inside. Mary Poppins said good night to Jack before following the group in.

In the front entry hall, Ellen watched the children

slink into the parlor. "Don't you be too 'ard on 'em, sir," Ellen told Michael. "They *are* just children, after all."

"Of course they're children," Michael snapped. "*My* children. And I will deal with them as I see fit. Now leave me to it."

"Yes, sir," Ellen said. She gave Mary Poppins a sympathetic glance before returning to the kitchen.

Mary Poppins moved toward the staircase, but Michael stopped her. "You too, Mary Poppins," he said, pointing toward the parlor.

Mary Poppins followed Michael into the parlor, where the children stood, heads hung low, awaiting sentence. Michael took a moment to get control over his anger before he spoke. "You could have lost me my job today," he said finally. "Do you understand that? A good position is hard to come by these days." He turned to Mary Poppins. "And *you*, Mary Poppins. I thought you came here to look after these children."

"It wasn't her doing," John said quickly. "It was us."

"We thought maybe if we talked to Mr. Frye, he could give you more time to save the house," Annabel explained.

"We were only trying to help," John said.

"Well, you didn't!" Michael shouted. He took a breath, trying to calm down. "I know this has been a difficult year for all of us, and I've tried my best to keep the three of you from worrying—but I can't do this alone. It's too much. I'm barely holding on as it is. I can't even remember my briefcase in the morning!" He ran a hand through his hair. "And there *is* no more time. We're about to lose our home. I just don't know what to do. Everything has fallen to pieces since your mother . . ." He paused, overcome with emotion. "Haven't we lost enough already?"

Georgie took Michael's hand. "We haven't lost Mother," he told his father. "Not really. As long as we remember her, she's still here."

"And up there," Annabel said, pointing out the window. There was a break in the fog, just enough to allow the light from a bright star to shine through the glass. "Watching over us."

Michael stared up at the star, too overwhelmed to speak. Annabel and Georgie wrapped their arms around him, and John soon joined in as well.

Michael hugged the three children tight and then let them go, wiping away a tear. "When did you all get so clever?" he asked.

"Last night," said Georgie. "Mary Poppins told us . . ." He stopped when he saw Mary Poppins raise a finger to her lips.

"I hope I know as much as you when I grow up," Michael told them. "And you're right. Your mother's not lost. She's in your smile, Georgie. And in John's walk, and Annabel's eyes. She'll always be with us wherever we go." Michael pulled the children close for another hug as Mary Poppins looked on, pleased.

"All right, now. Go on," he told the children. "Time to wash your hands for dinner."

Once the children had gone, Michael turned to face Mary Poppins. "Did you have something to do with them trying to save the house?" he asked.

"I never said a word," Mary Poppins insisted. "It was all the children's idea."

"The whole time I thought I'd been looking after them they'd been looking after me." Michael shook his head. "I had it all backwards."

Mary Poppins raised an eyebrow, a sly smile on her lips. "A Banks family trait," she said.

"What was I thinking?" Michael said, not listening. He seemed to have lost track of himself over the past couple of days, forgetting what was truly important.

"Some people think a great deal too much," Mary Poppins replied. "Of that I am certain."

This statement Michael heard. He watched Mary Poppins march to the hall and then up the stairs. She always seemed so confident, even when things were at their worst. She'd been just the same when he and Jane were children. How could she *know* things would work out, though? Had it just been a lucky guess before?

Michael had a hard time believing everything would be fine this time. There was simply no way to save the house. But he had his family, and as long as they were together, they'd have a *home*—wherever it was.

The family continued to search for the missing bank shares certificate while packing up the house. Michael rented a moving van to transport their belongings, and Georgie was relieved when he saw that the van looked nothing like the wagon the wolf had driven in the bowl. It was just a regular truck, with a large storage compartment in the back and no noisy steam engine. There was no sign of the evil wolf, either, or the greedy weasel and badger. Instead, Jack, Angus, and two of the other leeries helped the Bankses pack up the van. Although the items from the attic and most of the furniture would have to go into storage for now, Annabel and John had assured Georgie there was no danger of anything being stolen. His toys and clothes would all be going with him to Aunt Jane's, where the family would be living until they found a new home.

Outside, Jack and the leeries searched through each box before it was lifted into the van, in the hopes of finding the missing bank shares certificate. Jack spotted Jane emerging from the house, carrying another box, and he quickly jumped down to help her.

"Thank you," she said as Jack took the box. She nodded toward the truck. "Any luck?"

Jack glanced at Angus, who shook his head. Jane sighed. "We can look through everything again if you like," Jack offered.

"There's no point," Jane said. She knew it was a long shot, having searched through everything with Michael already. The box she'd just brought out was the last, and it contained only dishes. The certificate was gone. "It's nearly midnight," Jane continued. "We tried our best." She gave Jack a sad smile. "Thank you, Jack. And thanks to your friends for helping us."

"Of course," Jack said. "Anything for you." He blushed.

"We'll be out in a moment," Jane said shyly, blushing as well. How lucky she was—they all were—that Jack had come along when he did. She hoped he'd stay in their lives.

Jane returned inside and found Michael gazing around the empty parlor wistfully. "I suppose that's that," he said to her. He stared at the empty walls, dusty floor, and bare mantelpiece, remembering all they had done together in that room as a family. He could still feel Kate's presence, but he knew the children were right. Wherever they went, Kate would go with them. They wouldn't be leaving her behind.

Jane took her brother's arm and leaned her head against his shoulder. "This was a good home," she said softly. Michael nodded, unable to speak. Jane blinked back tears. She, too, had many, many happy memories of her time in the house with Michael and his family—and from the years before that, when Michael and Jane were young and shared the house with their own parents.

The sound of footsteps on the staircase broke through their thoughts. They each pulled out a hand-kerchief, quickly drying each other's tears with a laugh. By the time the children arrived at the bottom of the stairs, Jane and Michael were both calm, and they entered the front entrance hall with brave smiles on their faces, ready to greet Mary Poppins and the children.

"The children packed up the last of their things themselves." Mary Poppins nodded to the twins and Georgie, each of whom had a small suitcase at their feet.

"You have Gillie?" Michael asked Georgie. Georgie held up the stuffed giraffe.

Ellen emerged from the kitchen, carrying two suit-cases. "Good riddance to that bloomin' kitchen," Ellen said. "Never could figure out that stove."

"Well then," Michael said when everyone had their coats on and bags in hand. "It's time to go." He paused a moment and then tilted his head up. "Goodbye, old friend!" he called out.

"Goodbye, old friend!" Jane and the children shouted.

Their voices echoed through empty rooms. Michael opened the front door and they filed out one by one. Michael left last, turning out the lights as he went and shutting the door behind him.

Outside, the family was surprised to find a handful of neighbors and friends approaching number 17 from the admiral's house next door. Jack had conferred with Admiral Boom earlier, and Mr. Binnacle had alerted the others, who had gathered at the admiral's until the Bankses were ready to go.

In addition to Admiral Boom and his first mate, Miss Lark was there, with Willoughby, along with the milkman and a few of the other residents of Cherry Tree Lane.

"What are you all doing here so late?" Michael asked the group.

"We've been waitin' to see you off," Mr. Binnacle told him.

The milkman raised his cap in greeting. "We'd be here no matter what the hour," he said.

Miss Lark led Willoughby over to the children. Georgie and the twins scratched their favorite dog behind the ears and under his furry beard. "If you and your family should ever need a place to stay, Willoughby and I would be happy for the company," Miss Lark told Michael.

"That's very kind of you, Miss Lark," Michael said. "Jane has offered to put us up in her flat, at least for the time being."

Jane squeezed Michael's hand. "For as long as you like," she said, and then turned to Ellen. "I wish you'd come with us." Jane's flat was smaller than the Bankses' home, but she'd transformed all but the parlor and kitchen into bedrooms. It would be cozy, but she was certain she could make room for everyone.

"Don't you worry 'bout me," Ellen said to Jane. "I got a nice room fixed up at my sister's."

Annabel looked over at John, worried. They'd assumed they'd all be living together. If Ellen wasn't going with them, would they lose Mary Poppins as well? "You're not leaving us, are you, Mary Poppins?" Annabel asked the nanny.

"Don't be silly," said Mary Poppins.

"Your home is with us," Michael assured Mary Poppins. Jane nodded.

Georgie hadn't been worried, however. "She says she's not leaving until the door opens," he reminded his brother and sister. Annabel and John remembered Mary Poppins had said that, but they still didn't know what it meant.

"I'm glad she got caught on your string," Michael told Georgie with a smile.

The kite! Georgie had left it in the back of the closet and forgotten all about it. "My kite!" he cried, pulling on Michael's arm. "I have to go get it!"

"All right, but be quick about it," Michael said, unlocking the door. Georgie handed his suitcase and Gillie to his father and then dashed into the house.

While the family waited for Georgie, Mr. Binnacle pushed the admiral's wheelchair over to Michael. "The admiral has something he'd like to give you, Mr. Banks."

The admiral handed Michael a beautiful ship in a bottle. "The HMS *Glad Tidings*," Admiral Boom said. "I commanded her myself. May she guide you safely into port."

Michael held up the bottle, admiring the detail of the ship inside it. He glanced then at the admiral's roof, where the bow and front mast of the ship on the roof-deck were visible. He was impressed by the similarities between the admiral's life-size replica and the miniature version in his hand. "Thank you so much, Admiral." He raised his hand to his forehead in a salute. "I'll take good care of her."

Admiral Boom and Mr. Binnacle returned the salute, and the admiral checked his pocket watch. "It's nearly midnight, Mr. Binnacle," he told his first mate. "Time to man our posts."

"Yes, sir," replied Mr. Binnacle. "Goodbye, Mr. Banks, sir." Mr. Binnacle wheeled the admiral back to their house.

Georgie emerged from number 17 a moment later, holding up the kite. "I found it!" He ran over to show his father.

Michael smiled down at the patched kite. "I'm not sure that will get off the ground anymore," he said. "It looks more glue than kite." He peered more closely at it. "Are those patches from one of my old drawings?"

"You threw it out," Georgie said, pouting. He didn't think he should get in trouble for rescuing something from the rubbish.

"I'm not upset," Michael reassured his youngest. "It looks like you've done a fine job." He took the kite and studied it, smiling at the images of Kate and their children standing in front of their soon-to-be-former home. It would be a nice memento of their time there.

Michael then noticed what seemed to be writing on the back of one piece of the sketch. He held the kite up toward a streetlamp, letting the light shine on the paper from the back. He could now see printed lettering, upside down and backward, coming through the patches. Michael pieced together the words: CERTIFICATE . . . OF . . . SHARES.

CHAPTER

20

"The certificate of shares!" Michael said, waving the kite at the others. "This is it! What we've been looking for!" He turned to Jane. "We have to get to the bank! What time is it? Anyone?"

John quickly took out his pocket watch. "Seven minutes to midnight," he said.

"Seven minutes?" Michael sighed, defeated. "It's not enough time."

"Take the van," Jack suggested.

John shook his head, knowing that wouldn't speed things up enough. "Even driving, it's twelve minutes to the bank. You'd need another five and a half minutes to get there in time."

"There must be something we can do," Jane said.

"No, there's nothing," Michael replied. "We can't turn back time."

"Why not?" Annabel asked. She looked over at Mary Poppins hopefully. "'Everything is possible—even the *im*possible.'"

Mary Poppins smiled.

"Can we do it, Mary Poppins?" John asked. "Can we turn back time?"

"I don't see why that couldn't be arranged," Mary Poppins replied, her smile taking on a sly twinkle.

"That's ridiculous," Michael said.

"Indeed it is, Michael," Mary Poppins agreed. "It's nonsense."

"Foolishness," Annabel said.

"It makes no sense!" John declared, delighted. "And if it makes no sense . . ."

"It can't be true!" all three children yelled together.

"What are you all talking about?" Michael asked, confused.

"Never you mind," Mary Poppins told Michael. "You

just get to the bank as fast as possible with that kite. Leave the five and a half minutes to us."

Mary Poppins ushered Michael and Jane to the van. Michael climbed into the driver's seat while Jack helped Jane into the passenger side.

"But how will you . . ." Michael started.

"Go!" the children cried.

Michael glanced at Jane, who shrugged. It was always best not to argue with Mary Poppins. Michael started the engine.

Mary Poppins turned to Jack as the van sped away. "We'll need a lot of help," she told him.

"Good as done." Jack signaled to Angus and the other two leeries who had helped pack up the house, and the three men instantly hopped onto their bicycles and waited. With the twins' help, Jack then fashioned his ladder once again into a long passenger seat.

"I'll take the reins this time," Mary Poppins told Jack as she placed her hands on the handlebars. "Speed is of the essence."

"Have you ever ridden a bicycle like this before?" Jack asked her.

"Oh, please," Mary Poppins said dismissively. "How

different can it be from riding an elephant?" Jack grinned, and once all three children were settled in their seats, he joined the twins on the ladder.

"Ready?" Mary Poppins called out.

"Steady!" shouted the leeries.

Mary Poppins hiked up her skirt and hopped onto the bicycle seat sideways.

"*Go!*" yelled Georgie and the twins.

The four bicycles zoomed down Cherry Tree Lane, heading opposite the direction Jane and Michael had gone, with Mary Poppins in the lead.

John elbowed Annabel and pointed down to the pedals of Jack's bicycle. They were turning by themselves—without Mary Poppins's feet being on them! Jack had seen this as well, and the three shared a laugh. Mary Poppins's ability to propel a bicycle without pedaling might have been amazing, but it wasn't at all surprising: it had become impossible to be surprised by *anything* she did.

The streets were mostly empty at that point, and the *whoo*shomp-*whoo*shomp of the bike tires over the cobblestones echoed around them. They occasionally passed a car, or a worker walking home from a late-night job who would stare in curiosity at the odd caravan.

Eventually, Mary Poppins led the leeries onto the Victoria Embankment. John, seated on the outside of the ladder, closest to the River Thames, could see the flickering globes of the streetlamps reflected in the still water, and he smiled at the beautiful sight.

Annabel was looking ahead, however, where ground lights illuminated the base of Buckingham Palace, the home of King George and Queen Mary. It was strange to imagine the king and queen sleeping soundly in their beds, unaware of the strange bike-riding pack speeding past their majestic home.

The group veered right onto the wide mall in front of the palace. As they did, more leeries appeared on their bicycles, coming from all directions. Soon there were two dozen leeries following behind Mary Poppins as she steered Jack's bicycle—without using her hands, which were folded in her lap—toward the Houses of Parliament.

At the far end of the large structure was the House of Commons, which sat next to a grand clock tower.

There Mary Poppins slowed the bicycle to a stop. The rest of the leeries quickly hit their brakes, coming to a stop as well.

John recognized the gigantic clock that gazed out from the top of the tower. He had never been that close to Big Ben. He stared up at it, awed and speechless. This was the clock that made sure all of London knew the time. And now Big Ben was going to help them *turn back* time so that his father and Aunt Jane could get to the bank by midnight.

Minutes after the children had climbed down from the bike, they were climbing *up*, ascending a tall ladder Angus had created by tying together Jack's ladder and his own with a rope he'd brought along. The ladder had been set against the wall on the far end of the House of Commons, in the gap between Parliament and the clock tower. The rest of the leeries followed, each carrying his own ladder.

Once the group had reached the roof, Jack and Angus pulled up the double ladder, which they tipped across the gap to the clock tower. The tower was three times as tall as Parliament, however, and the top of the double ladder landed only midway up it. But this was where the other ladders would come in handy.

The children watched as Jack began to climb the double ladder, with the leeries following. When Jack reached the top of the ladder, the leerie below him passed up another ladder. Jack balanced this new ladder atop the ladder he was on, leaning it against the wall of the tower, and then carefully climbed again.

John held his breath as Jack repeated the process. John knew gravity and pressure were keeping the ladders in place, but the slightest shift could tip one of the ladders out of alignment, and Jack and the leeries would come crashing down.

Angus handed Jack the last ladder and Jack raised it over his head. He leaned it against the tower, but the top landed several feet below the clockface.

Jack groaned. They were a ladder short. He glanced down over his shoulder, and he could just make out Mary Poppins and the children, staring up at him, in the dim moonlight. Even that high up, he could see the hopeful expressions on the faces of the children and the calm confidence in Mary Poppins's encouraging smile. He couldn't let them down—he *wouldn't* let them down.

A bright star in the sky blinked on and sent a soft

beam down toward the street, where the leeries' bicy-cles were lined up. They looked from that distance like tiny toys.

When Jack saw the bicycles, the solution hit him: putting the ladder sideways, like he'd done on his bike! He took down the ladder above him and then balanced it across the top of the ladder he was standing on.

Angus had figured out what Jack was up to, and he climbed up behind Jack, reaching around his friend to grab one end of the perpendicular ladder, holding tight as Jack slowly climbed along the rungs to the opposite end.

Below, the children had realized what Jack was up to as well, and they watched, tense and worried, as he crawled to the end of the ladder. Georgie hugged Gillie tightly. John clutched his pocket watch for good luck. Annabel put her hands over her eyes. "I can't watch!" she cried.

Only Mary Poppins remained calm. She even rolled her eyes at the drama of it all. "You'd think they'd never done this before," she commented.

Above them, Jack carefully stood up. "Now!" he called down to Angus. Angus yanked on the far end of the ladder, propelling Jack into the air, up to the glowing face of the clock dial—where he landed safely on the ledge. Below, the children let out a mutual sigh of relief.

Jack opened a hinged window set into the face of the clock. It was just big enough for a man to squeeze through. And that was exactly what Jack did, crawling in and then standing up and looking around, taking in the impressive clockwork. The space rose three stories high, with two levels of multiple gears, large and small. The bells hung high above the gears, at the very top of the tower.

There was one great bell, twice as big as Jack, which tolled out the hour—and it was this bell that was the true Big Ben. There were also four bells nearly as big as Big Ben that chimed only on the quarter hour.

The clockwork was run by gravity, via a long pendulum that descended through the middle of the tower. Jack shivered in the cold as he made his way around the gears, searching for the gas main that lit the clockface at night. He finally spotted the wheel that kept the pipe open. In the same way that a leerie dimmed the gas in the streetlamps each morning by lowering the flames,

Jack cranked the giant wheel. That would dim the light in the clockface, preventing anyone from seeing what time it was.

Dimming the light would also prevent anyone from seeing if the time was being changed.

CHAPTER
21

While Jack was inside the clock tower, Mr. Wilkins was safe and warm in front of his office fireplace at the bank, watching the minute hand on his pocket watch inch its way toward the hour. Once both hands lined straight up at twelve, it would be midnight, and the Bankses' house would be his.

Mr. Wilkins turned to Mr. Gooding and Mr. Frye, who were waiting in the office with him. "Looks like Banks won't be joining us tonight," he said to the lawyers. None of the men were looking out the window behind

Mr. Wilkins's desk, so they didn't notice when the four faces of the distant clock tower went dark.

"Mr. Banks does have a few more minutes," Mr. Frye said to Mr. Wilkins. "You promised you'd wait until the last stroke of midnight."

"I know that," Mr. Wilkins said, irritated. "We'll wait. I'm a man of my word." There was now less than a minute left. He propped up the open pocket watch on the fireplace's mantel, and all three men kept their eyes glued on the second hand as it ticked down its last seconds to midnight.

Outside the window, in the distance, a tiny figure holding an umbrella magically descended from the sky, grabbing hold of Big Ben's minute hand.

Mr. Wilkins, eyes still on the watch, began to count down. "Four . . . three . . ."

At the same time, the figure with the umbrella pulled the minute hand backward—by one minute, then two.

"Two . . ." Mr. Wilkins continued. "One . . . and . . ." He straightened up and listened, waiting for Big Ben's great bell to toll. He frowned, puzzled. "Why hasn't Big Ben chimed?" he demanded. He crossed to his desk and glanced out the window. "The clock has gone dark!"

The lawyers hurried over to join him. As they did, the clockface once again lit up. "Ah!" Mr. Gooding said, pushing up his glasses and pointing out the window. "They've relit it."

"But that time is wrong," Mr. Wilkins said.

"Perhaps your watch is running fast," Mr. Frye suggested.

"Don't be a simpleton," Mr. Wilkins snapped. "My watch has never run fast. The clock must have stopped."

Mr. Frye was about to argue, but Mr. Gooding silenced him with a sharp shake of the head.

Meanwhile, Mr. Wilkins noticed a van pulling up on the street below. The driver's door opened and a young man stepped out. "Banks is here!" Mr. Wilkins cried.

Mr. Frye smiled in relief. "He's made it in time!"

Mr. Wilkins spun around to glare at Mr. Frye. "Not *yet* he hasn't. Go down there and see he doesn't get inside until that blasted clock strikes twelve."

"But, sir—" Mr. Frye protested.

"Now!" Mr. Wilkins ordered the lawyers.

Mr. Gooding grabbed Mr. Frye's arm and dragged him out to the hall.

Outside, on the street below, Michael grabbed the kite from the van, and he and Jane dashed up the stairs to the front door of the bank. They pushed on the handles, but the door wouldn't budge. "It must be locked," Michael told Jane, not able to see the two lawyers who had made it downstairs and were pushing from inside against the door to keep it closed.

Michael knocked on the glass. "Please, someone!" he yelled through the crack in the door. "Let us in!" He leaned back and yelled up to the windows above. "We have to get in!" He waited a moment, but there was no answer.

Michael glanced at the kite in his hands and got an idea. He gestured for Jane to follow him as he darted back down the stairs and around to the side of the building. He could now see the light coming from Mr. Wilkins's office. He handed Jane the kite and then stepped backward, holding the string. Jane angled the kite and it caught a current of wind, flying out of her hands and soaring up to Mr. Wilkins's window. Michael knew that unless Mr. Wilkins was looking out the window, he wouldn't see the kite.

"We need to get it inside," Jane told Michael. He

nodded in agreement. But how could they get the kite to go through a closed window?

A figure floated into view above them, holding an umbrella. Mary Poppins! The nanny inhaled deeply, then gently blew, creating a strong breeze. The windows of Mr. Wilkins's office flew open. The kite broke free of its string and sailed in.

Inside, Mr. Wilkins had returned to his desk, but the kite had found its mark, hitting him in the back of his head before landing on his desk—just as Big Ben began to toll midnight. Mr. Wilkins stared down at the kite, bewildered. It had landed facedown, permitting Mr. Wilkins to read the words "Certificate of Shares" on the back of one of the patches.

Outside, Jane and Michael raced back to the front door of the bank. They pushed harder this time, but Mr. Gooding and Mr. Frye were still leaning on the door from the inside, keeping it from budging.

Mr. Frye was overcome with shame at the deception they were carrying out. "I'm sorry, I'm sorry," he murmured to himself. Finally, he could stand it no longer. He let go of the door and stepped back, causing Mr. Gooding to lose his grip—and his balance. Mr. Gooding tumbled sideways, his eyeglasses flying off, as Michael and Jane pushed open the door and rushed inside.

"Thank you so much for letting us in!" Michael said, helping Mr. Gooding up and handing him his eyeglasses. Michael had assumed the men had kindly unlocked the door for them.

Before Mr. Gooding could correct them, Mr. Frye gestured to the siblings urgently. "Hurry!" he cried. Big Ben had continued to toll and there was no time to spare.

As Jane and Michael raced up the stairs, Mr. Frye saw a bicycle speed onto the street outside and stop in front of the bank. Its four passengers jumped off the bike; Mr. Frye instantly recognized the three smallest as the Banks children. He held the door open for the group, sharing a smile with Georgie as the children ran in, followed by Jack. Mr. Frye waved the group toward the stairs and they hurried on.

He was about to close the door, but at that moment it seemed to push itself open. He let go of the handle and the door remained open as Mary Poppins stepped in, smiling politely at the two dumbfounded lawyers before calmly striding across the lobby floor toward the others.

Upstairs, meanwhile, Michael and Jane arrived in Mr. Wilkins's office, where the bank president still sat, stunned, with the kite now in his hands.

"That's it!" Michael said, pointing to the kite. "Our bank shares certificate!" At that moment, Big Ben gonged its final note. There then followed a distant boom, coming from a rooftop in another part of town.

Jane smiled to herself. She could imagine Admiral Boom was pleased that Big Ben had finally matched the admiral's timekeeping.

Michael took the kite from Mr. Wilkins and peeled off the patches. The children raced in, and Jane waved them over as Michael arranged the pieces of the certificate on Mr. Wilkins's desk. Jack quietly entered next, and Jane gave him a grateful smile. He nodded modestly, as if to say, *It was the least I could do.*

Mary Poppins strolled in, followed by the lawyers. Mr. Gooding crept in meekly, relieved that Mr. Wilkins, eyes glued to the certificate, didn't seem to notice them. Mr. Frye was unafraid, however. Helping Michael had changed him somehow, and his former timidity had vanished. He'd discovered that it felt much more powerful to help someone than to harm them.

"And this one goes here," Michael said as he arranged another piece.

"Does it matter if it's cut to bits?" Jane asked.

"It's valid so long as all the pieces are there," Mr. Frye said quickly before Mr. Wilkins could reply. Mr. Wilkins glared at him, but Mr. Frye glared right back, causing Mr. Wilkins to blink in shock.

When Michael had finished, there was still one piece missing. Michael examined both sides of the kite, but there were no more patches left. He turned to Georgie. "There was one more bit. A corner piece with a lot of signatures. Do you remember it?"

Georgie nodded. "I didn't need that part," he told his father. "I threw it away." Georgie saw his father's shoulders slump. "I'm sorry, Father."

Michael put his arm around his youngest son. "It's all right."

"It's *not* all right," announced Mr. Wilkins. He stood up behind the desk, smiling in triumph. "Without those signatures, you have no bank shares. No house. You have *nothing*."

Michael stared at Mr. Wilkins, stunned by the bank president's obvious glee.

"But he knows you have bank shares!" Annabel protested.

"He's been planning this all along," John told his father. He and Annabel had been proven right in their suspicions—but it was the worst thing that could've happened.

"Take your children out of here, Banks," Mr. Wilkins ordered Michael, pointing to the door. "I've heard enough of their lies."

Michael's eyes blazed with anger. "Don't you dare insult my children," he said. "They're not lying and you know it. I only wish I had believed them sooner." Michael turned to the children. "You had him pegged right from the start. I'm sorry I didn't believe you." He wrapped his arms around them and glared over their shoulders at Mr. Wilkins. "Take the house," he said. "Go ahead. I have all I need right here." Mary Poppins smiled at Michael, pleased.

"He has you there, Willie," came a voice from the doorway. The children glanced behind them as an elderly man entered the office. It was the man in the portrait above the fireplace! He was much older now but with the same friendly smile and the same kind twinkle in his eyes as in the painting. Despite being in his eighties, he still had a youthfulness and lightness of spirit that the much younger Mr. Wilkins lacked.

"Uncle Dawes?" Mr. Wilkins said in shock. "What on earth are you doing here?"

"A little bird told me you've been trying to cheat the Banks family out of their shares in the Fidelity Fiduciary," Mr. Dawes, Jr., said. He exchanged sly winks with the parrot on Mary Poppins's umbrella. "I also hear you've been telling the whole of Westminster I've gone loony." His smile faded and he glared at his nephew. "The only loony thing I did was trust you to look after this bank."

"But I've nearly doubled its profits!" Mr. Wilkins protested.

"By wringing it out of our customers' pockets," replied Mr. Dawes, Jr. "Their trust in us built this bank—and now you've squandered every last bit of their goodwill. And so I'm back." Mr. Dawes, Jr., crossed the room and took his place behind the desk, ushering Mr. Wilkins to the side. "And you're out." Mr. Dawes, Jr., nodded to Mr. Gooding and Mr. Frye. "See my nephew to the door, would you, gentlemen?"

"Yes, sir, Mr. Dawes, Jr.," Mr. Frye said enthusiastically. He gestured to Mr. Gooding. They stepped over to Mr. Wilkins and grabbed his arms.

Mr. Wilkins struggled to free himself. "Get your hands off me!" he demanded, but Mr. Frye tightened his grip. "You're not fit to run this bank!" Mr. Wilkins shouted to his uncle as the lawyers dragged him out.

Mr. Dawes, Jr., laughed. "We'll see about that," he said. He turned to Michael and the others. "I may be getting on in years, but I still have a few steps left in me."

He emerged from behind the desk and kicked out one leg, brushing the toe of his shoe onto the tile floor—*swish*. He brought down the heel—*clack*. He repeated this move with the other foot and then repeated both again. Within seconds he was tap-dancing around the room. As he danced past Mary Poppins, he held out his hand to her. Mary Poppins gave her umbrella to Jack and joined the old—and now *new*—bank president in a soft-shoe routine while the Bankses clapped out a rhythm.

Finally, Mr. Dawes, Jr., twirled Mary Poppins away from him—but he was hardly through! He then leapt up onto his desk and performed an energetic solo before hopping down and landing in his chair behind the desk.

He leaned back, a huge grin lighting up his face and erasing years from his age.

The others applauded. "So glad to have you back, Mr. Dawes, Jr.," Michael told him.

"Thank you, son," Mr. Dawes, Jr., replied. "And by the way, those shares of yours are perfectly fine. There's no need to cash them in. Save them for your family."

"I don't understand," Michael said.

Mr. Dawes, Jr., gestured for Georgie and the twins to approach his desk. "I have a little story for you, children," he said. "Once upon a time, there was a little boy named Michael who wanted to give his tuppence to a bird lady." Mr. Dawes, Jr., smiled at Michael. "But in the end, he decided it was more important to give the money to his father. His father—*your* grandfather—gave those tuppence to this bank and asked us to guard them well. We did just that. And thanks to several clever investments, those tuppence have grown into quite a sum."

Michael and Jane exchanged looks of shock. "Really?" Michael asked.

Mr. Dawes, Jr., grinned. "Really, Michael. Enough, in fact, to pay off that loan you took and still have plenty left. The house is yours."

CHAPTER

22

The children woke up the next morning and looked out the window of Jane's flat to discover spring had arrived. Cherry trees rustled in the breeze, flourishing with new blossoms. Because it had been so late when they left the bank, Michael had gratefully accepted an offer from the leeries to drive the moving van back to number 17 and unload the furniture and boxes. When the family returned home, after one night away, they could immediately begin to unpack.

Jane called Ellen to tell her the news, and the house-keeper insisted on coming over and making breakfast for everyone. After their meal, the family finally set out for home.

Michael took a deep breath as they stepped outside Jane's residence. "What a beautiful day to be going back home again," he said.

Jane gestured to the trees. "You should paint this, Michael," she said.

Michael smiled at his sister as they started down the street. "I will, Jane. I will." For the first time in a year, he felt inspired. He wouldn't put his art supplies back in the attic, he decided. He'd set them up in the home's spare room and make it his studio.

They headed home and reached the gates of their old neighborhood park, where they saw colorful tents set up in the center of the green, along with a small Ferris wheel. Crowds were lined up to buy treats and try their luck at games of chance.

"The spring fair!" John said. "It's today!" He turned to his father. "Can we go?" The children looked at Michael pleadingly.

Michael grinned. "I don't see why not." A fair celebrating the new season seemed the perfect way to celebrate all that had happened over the past few days.

He expected the children to run ahead, but instead Georgie grabbed his left hand, and Annabel his right.

"Come on, Father!" Annabel said, tugging on his hand. John ran behind Michael and pushed him forward.

Michael laughed and shrugged helplessly at Jane as his children propelled him into the park.

Mary Poppins paused at the entrance and watched as the family hurried ahead, their voices fading until they had blended in with the music and jovial sounds from the fair. A knowing look appeared in her eyes and a pleased look on her face. She nodded to herself in approval.

Michael and the others didn't notice Mary Poppins was no longer with them. They were too busy taking in the sights. The park was filled with familiar faces, including those of the friends who had gathered the night before outside their house to wish them well. Mr. Binnacle pushed Admiral Boom in his wheelchair toward a stand selling flags, and the milkman chatted with a baker selling fresh biscuits. Georgie spotted Miss Lark; he dashed over to pet Willoughby and fill Miss Lark in on what had happened at the bank.

John nudged Annabel and nodded toward the

park-keeper, who was standing beneath a tree, glowering as the crowds trampled over his grass. The twins exchanged amused glances and giggled.

"Will you go on the Ferris wheel with us?" John asked his father.

"Of course!" Michael said. "You should have a go, too, Jane," he told his sister.

Jane grabbed Ellen's arm. "Only if Ellen comes with me," she said with a grin.

Ellen tried to pull away. "I wouldn't be caught dead on that thing." Jane latched on more tightly and tugged her along.

Georgie rejoined the group, and as they approached the Ferris wheel, they heard a tune begin to play nearby. They glanced around, attempting to see where it was coming from.

"Balloons!" Georgie pointed toward a bouquet of colorful balloons tied to a wheeled cart. The tune they'd heard was coming from a small pipe organ sitting on top of the cart. On the bench next to the cart sat an old woman wearing a hat made up of crocheted flowers that matched the bright colors of the balloons.

Georgie gazed up at his father. "May we have bal-loons?" he asked.

"Of course we can," Michael replied. He grabbed the hands of the twins while Jane took Georgie's. They raced across the grass toward the cart.

"Wait! 'Ere! 'Ere!" the park-keeper shouted after them. The family ignored him, and when they neared the cart, they heard the balloon lady singing along to the street organ's tune. She smiled as the Banks children approached.

Michael held out several coins to the balloon lady. "We'd like some of your very finest balloons, please," he told her.

"That you shall have," the old woman replied. "But choose carefully, my dearie ducks. Many have picked the wrong balloon. Be sure to choose the one that's right for you."

"Which one would you like?" Michael asked Georgie.

Georgie hesitated, afraid of making a mistake and picking the wrong one.

"Why don't you go first, sir?" the balloon lady told Michael.

Michael glanced at the balloon lady, startled. "Me?" he asked. "I don't think I've held a balloon since I was a child."

The balloon lady's eyes twinkled with the wisdom of the elderly. "Ah," she said. "Then you've forgotten what it's like."

Michael laughed. "What it's like to hold a balloon?"

The balloon lady shook her head. "To be a child." She tilted her head toward the balloon bouquet. "Choose wisely," she repeated. Michael shrugged, finding the whole conversation quite silly, but when he reached into the bouquet, the string of a purple balloon seemed to slip into his palm, as if to say, *Pick me!*

Michael took the cue and plucked out the purple balloon. Inside the balloon was a hazy image, which crystallized, becoming the face of a little boy—a very *familiar* little boy: it was Michael himself as a child. He turned to Jane, and when he saw her astonished expression, he knew she could see it, too.

Michael felt a tug: the balloon was rising. It kept rising, and rising some more. Michael's arm stretched high over his head, and as he held on tight, his feet lifted off the ground.

"Michael!" Jane called up to her brother as he kept ascending.

Michael laughed, elated. "I remember!" he yelled down to his sister. "It's all true! Every impossible thing we imagined with Mary Poppins—it all happened!"

Georgie and the twins stared at their father, floating above them and laughing, looking happier than he had in months. Michael waved at the children with his free hand, beckoning them to join him.

Georgie quickly grabbed a light blue balloon, the color of the cloudless sky above them, and he, too, soon rose, shrieking in glee. The twins eagerly plucked their own balloons: Annabel took hold of a sunny yellow one, and John snared a bright green one that looked like the new leaves on the park's trees.

Jane watched as Michael and the children sailed over the crowd, kicking their legs and laughing. She wanted to join them, but she was hesitant about which balloon to pick. None seemed to call to her, at least not that she could tell.

"This one looks like you," she heard someone say. A hand reached over her shoulder to take a balloon.

Jane turned to find Jack, now holding a pink balloon.

Jane gazed into the balloon and saw, as Michael had a few moments before, a cloudy image of her younger self. "How did you know?" she asked Jack as she took the balloon from him. Before he could answer, the balloon lifted her into the air.

"Don't you lose her, son!" Jack heard Admiral Boom shout. Mr. Binnacle pushed the admiral's chair across the grass toward the cart.

"I won't, sir!" Jack replied with a salute; he quickly grabbed a bright blue balloon and sailed off after Jane.

Once his first mate had wheeled him close enough, Admiral Boom chose a balloon for himself. Inside he saw an image of a little boy in a sailor suit. The admiral grinned, unaware he had been lifted out of his wheel-chair. "Masts and mizzens! I've set sail!" he cried when he finally noticed. "Chart a course, Mr. Binnacle!"

"That I will, sir!" Mr. Binnacle quickly picked his own balloon and rose next to his commander.

Ellen, not wanting to be left behind, snatched an aqua balloon and took off, soon joining the others.

The balloon lady noticed three serious-looking men in suits making their way toward her cart. One looked very much like a banker, and she watched him peer around at the festivities suspiciously, as if the genuine joy he saw around him was somehow improper. The expressions on the other two men's faces were wary yet intrigued, which led the balloon lady to conclude that they were lawyers.

The two lawyers came to her first. Mr. Frye reached for a balloon. Mr. Gooding shook his head in disapproval. Mr. Frye, however, ignored his colleague and plucked out a pretty orange balloon. Inside the balloon, he noticed the smiling face of his younger self, nodding in encouragement. He raised the balloon over his head. He'd seen the Banks family rise from the ground with their balloons, and he was quite pleased when he was able to do the same.

Mr. Gooding, horrified by Mr. Frye's frivolous behavior, grabbed on to his colleague's leg, intending to drag him back to earth. Instead, Mr. Gooding rose. He clutched tightly to Mr. Frye's leg as the two men sailed toward where the Banks family had ascended.

Mr. Wilkins, the third person, watched the lawyers fly off; he was flabbergasted.

"Would you like to try one yourself, sir?" the balloon lady asked him.

Mr. Wilkins frowned down at the old woman. What a ridiculous idea. He was about to tell her off but then hesitated. If Michael Banks could fly, surely someone of Mr. Wilkins's stature could fly even higher. "Why not," he said finally. "I'll give it a go."

The balloon lady nodded toward the balloons. "All right, love," she said. "But be sure to choose carefully."

Mr. Wilkins didn't need to be lectured on how to pick a balloon, especially not by an old lady. He snatched the nearest balloon and raised it into the sky, waiting to be lifted off. Instead, the balloon slowly sank to the ground.

The balloon lady shrugged. "You know what they say, love. There are a lot of ups and downs in life. Your 'up' may come again." Mr. Wilkins scowled, not at all comforted by the balloon lady's words. He was soon shoved aside by the crowd, eager to claim their own balloons.

Shortly after, the sky was filled with park-goers, each holding a brightly colored balloon. Miss Lark flew up with Willoughby, whose balloon was tied to his collar. The milkman waved to Miss Lark as he glided past her, holding a milk-colored balloon. Even the park-keeper joined in, an uncharacteristic grin on his face as his grass-green balloon carried him high over his workplace.

The park emptied out, leaving only the balloon lady and Mary Poppins, who stood alone near the entrance, watching the balloon- and people-filled sky.

The balloon lady left her cart and made her way to Mary Poppins, who smiled in greeting. "Of course, the grown-ups will all forget by tomorrow," the balloon lady told her friend.

Mary Poppins nodded. "They always do," she said.

"Only one balloon left, Mary Poppins." The balloon lady held out a red balloon. "I think it must be yours."

"I suppose it must," Mary Poppins agreed. Inside the balloon, an image stared back at her, identical in age and dress to the Mary Poppins of the present. She smiled in approval. "Practically perfect in every way," she said.

The balloons carried the Banks family, along with Ellen, to Cherry Tree Lane and then descended to the street.

Michael waved his arm toward number 17 once they had landed. "Welcome home, everyone!" he said.

After handing her balloon to Jane, Ellen marched up the steps to the door and ripped down the REPOSSESSION notice. She tore it into bits and tossed the pieces into the air. They rained down like confetti. The children applauded and Ellen took a quick bow.

"It's nice to be back, isn't it?" Jane said to Michael.

"It is," he said. "I never thought I'd feel this much joy and wonder ever again. I thought that door was closed to me forever."

A strong gust of wind suddenly blew down the street toward them. It swirled through the cherry blossoms, filling the sky with pink petals, and then sailed to the front door of number 17, pushing it wide open.

The open doorway beckoned the children, who assumed Mary Poppins was inside, to enter. After losing sight of her in the park, they'd concluded that she had returned to the house to begin unpacking things.

"Let's show Mary Poppins our balloons," Annabel told her brothers as she dashed past Ellen and headed into the house. John and Georgie followed, balloons in hand, calling out for Mary Poppins.

Mary Poppins was still in the park, however. The balloon lady and the other vendors had left. She was alone. The same wind that had blown down Cherry Tree Lane now rustled through the park's trees, sending cherry blossoms cascading around her. The wind tugged on her balloon, and the string slipped from her fingers. She watched as it sailed off into the sky, toward the clouds gathering overhead.

"It's time," Mary Poppins said to herself, picking up her carpetbag. She opened her umbrella, raising it up until it caught the breeze and lifted her into the air.

At the same time, Michael and Jane stood on the stoop outside number 17 and watched the cherry blossoms swirl overhead, carried by the strong breeze sweeping around them. The wind was a familiar one, and they knew what it meant.

"She's gone, hasn't she?" Jane said to her brother.

Michael nodded. "Thank you, Mary Poppins," he said quietly into the air. "Goodbye."

High above, unseen by Michael or Jane, Mary Poppins sailed over their home again on Cherry Tree Lane. She hovered a moment and smiled down at the brother and sister, pleased she had been able to help them again. She then tilted her umbrella to catch the breeze and soared up into the clouds.

In another part of London, as Jack stopped to retie his balloon to his bicycle, he noticed a tiny figure floating overhead. He smiled and tipped his cap. "*I* won't forget the magic of these past days, Mary Poppins," he said softly. "I promise." He climbed onto his bike and pedaled home.